THE FAERIE RACE BOOK THREE

THE DOOMSDAY TRIAL

CLAIRE LUANA
J.A. ARMITAGE

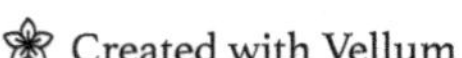 Created with Vellum

1

I thought I'd been ready for the Fantastic Faerie Race. I thought I'd been ready for whatever I'd find over the Hedge in Faerwild, for the tests and challenges, even a little not-so-friendly competition. But the last few weeks had shown me how horribly, naively wrong I had been.

The race competitors had been trained for physical strength, for intellect, even our magical capabilities had been honed. But no one had prepared me for the emotional toll this race would take.

No one had even asked me how I would cope if someone were to die. No one had asked me what I'd do if my sister suddenly reappeared out of nowhere...and not a single producer or staffer had asked how I'd cope emotionally with the ever-present threat of my own demise.

There'd been talk of how dangerous it would be. We'd been warned to watch our backs, but I'd thought it was just the studio trying to scare us to make great TV. I hadn't believed anyone would really get hurt in here, much less killed—and yet, I'd seen three people involved in this godforsaken race die in a matter of weeks.

I gazed up at the ornate ceiling of one of the Faerie king's palace guest suites, these thoughts refusing to leave, my sorrow shredding at my heart with vicious swipes.

Orin's warm arm snaked over me, pulling me closer to him. I yielded to him, snuggling closer. In what felt like a sea of desolation, he was my only life preserver. If it hadn't been for Orin, I'd have completely lost it.

The palace staff had assigned us both rooms, but I'd followed Orin to his and curled up in his arms, adrift in my misery. Neither of us had bothered to undress, both of us falling into bed in the wetsuit-like FFR outfits we'd been wearing since we'd started the final leg of the Elemental Trial. Orin had fallen asleep first, his deep rhythmic breathing keeping me company as I counted down the minutes to midnight.

I hadn't been able to sleep a wink, despite the exhaustion weighing me down like a stone. How could I? If Ben's senseless death wasn't enough to keep me awake, the thought that I was finally going to see my sister after two years of searching kept my eyelids firmly open.

I'd read Cass's note so many times in the half-light of the moon that I knew every curve of every letter, and yet, I held onto it, fearful if I let go, it would somehow magically disappear. Taking Cass with it.

Come to the Goddess of the Moon at midnight. Bring Orin. - Cass.

That was all it said.

Outside a bell chimed. I counted the chimes as I had at every hour since we'd collapsed on the bed. Eleven.

I didn't want to, but I shuffled out from beneath the safety and warmth of Orin's arm and headed to the en suite bathroom. I unzipped the oversized FFR hoodie Orin had put on me while we waited on the beach, shivering and numb. I didn't even know who it belonged to. As I dropped it to the floor, something fell out of one of the pockets. Picking it up, I saw it was a small black leather roll, tied with ribbon. I untied it and found that when the leather lay flat, it formed a black mask, the kind that would go over your eyes for a masquerade ball. And what was more—there were two of them, one laid neatly on top of the other.

I furrowed my brow, holding them up. Where had they come from? Did they belong to the prior owner of this hoodie, or had Cass slipped these in my pocket with the note? If so, why?

Too drained to solve the mystery now, I lay the masks on the counter and showered quickly, washing the salt and sand from my body. Then, wrapping a towel around me, I headed back into the bedroom. Orin was still asleep. He was so heart-wrenchingly beautiful with his dark hair falling over his eyes, yet his sleeping face was contorted with worry. I hardly had it in my heart to wake him, but he was finding no peace in his dreams, and there was no way I was going to leave the palace on my own. Besides, in her note, Cass had specifically asked me to bring him.

I nudged him lightly, and he stirred.

His black-as-night eyes fixated on mine, and I became acutely aware that I was wearing nothing more than a towel. Orin grabbed my hand and pulled me towards him, bringing me into a kiss that shattered me to my very core. It wasn't a kiss of passion but of hope, of safety, of comfort. And yet, the touch of his lips upon mine brought tears to my eyes which fell between us, wetting both of our cheeks.

"Don't tell me my kissing is that atrocious," Orin said, rubbing a thumb across my cheek to wipe away the tears.

"The worst." I smiled, running a hand through his silken

hair. I couldn't quite believe I got to touch him now, that this was allowed. "It's eleven."

Orin nodded. "I have an idea of how to get past the guards. You get dressed, while I have a quick shower and I'll fill you in." He walked over to the bathroom, and a few seconds later, the sound of rushing water hit my ears.

Padding over to the one wardrobe in the room, I opened it to find a couple of FFR outfits, both in Orin's size, a suit and a couple of pairs of jeans and t-shirts.

I guessed that if I'd have slept in my room, my wardrobe would have had clothes tailored to me. But I didn't want anyone catching me sneaking down the corridor and questioning my motives for being out so late, so I pulled out one of the t-shirts and a pair of jeans and slipped into them. The jeans hung off me, but I found a belt to hold them up. I wouldn't win any fashion awards, that was for sure, but it didn't matter what I wore. It only mattered that I was going to see Cass.

Sitting on the bed, I fidgeted while waiting for Orin. I couldn't keep still. The minutes were ticking down, and though Orin had assured me he knew exactly where the "Goddess of the Moon" was, we still had to get past the guards and plan or no plan, it would take time. Time I couldn't afford. When the bathroom door finally opened, I heaved a sigh of relief and stood, but no one came out.

"Orin?" I padded to the bathroom, sneaking a look inside, but it was empty. "Orin?" I whispered again, the fear beginning to creep up inside me. Had they managed to take Orin somehow? It was impossible. I'd been watching the bathroom door out of the corner of my eye the whole time.

"I'm here."

I jumped in shock at the voice in my ear and turned, throwing an elbow into something solid.

"Ow! You hit me." Orin materialized in front of me, clutching his stomach.

"Sorry," I said, shaking my head. What the hell had just happened? "You were right there, and I didn't see you. Why didn't I see you?"

Orin's eyes crinkled at the edges, and a mischievous grin spread across his face. "It was my fault. You didn't see me because I was wearing this." He held up one of the leather masks I'd abandoned in the bathroom earlier.

"You're a master of disguise," I countered, still not taking his point. What did a cheesy masquerade mask have to do with this?

"You don't get it, do you?" Orin held the mask up and put it back on his face. Within a second he'd vanished completely.

I stumbled back a step. "Holy shit. You're invisible."

He pulled the mask off, reappearing again. "I found them in the bathroom. There are two of them. I was planning to try to put the guards to sleep, but this is much better."

"They fell out of my pocket when I was getting undressed. They must have been with the letter from Cass," I said, growing excited. "She thought of everything! A way to help us get out of the palace, undetected!"

Now that the shock of elbowing an invisible Orin in the stomach wore off, and the surprise of the invisibility masks had subsided a little, I grew keenly aware that Orin was completely naked—save for a white fluffy towel wrapped around his waist. His bare chest was lean and chiseled, his abs rippling downward in a perfect V, his strong arms roped with muscle. He probably didn't even have to do sit-ups, damn faerie metabolism. His pale skin looked like marble on a statue, and I longed to reach out and touch it. But a wave of shyness hit me as I realized how quickly we'd been breaking through the walls between us. It was all a little overwhelming. "You better get dressed," I managed, clearing my scratchy throat.

The glint in Orin's eye suggested that he knew just what my line of thought had been, but he stayed blessedly quiet. He dressed quickly, dropping the towel to the floor as he pulled on his pants. I found myself wishing he was wearing the mask because watching him was almost unbearable. His body was achingly beautiful and I'd finally seen it in all its glory, albeit for half a second while he dressed.

I needed to get my mind out of the gutter and onto more important things—like getting out of the palace and meeting Cass. I looked at my watch. It was already half past eleven. Sucking in a deep breath, I threw my thoughts of Orin's naked body to one side and began to pull on my shoes.

We tied the masks onto our faces, and Orin vanished once more. It was strange, when I looked down I could see myself like normal. "Did it work?" I asked. I felt a ghostly hand fumble along my side, searching for my own.

"It worked." Clinging tightly to each other, we headed out of the bedroom door and into the palace.

2

———

The Faerie king's palace was a huge austere behemoth filled with long empty hallways. Orin's room had been sparsely furnished, but there had been a few cozy touches—a plush carpet, a pot holding a strange night-blooming plant.

The palace itself seemed empty, as if the Faerie king hadn't taken the time to furnish the cavernous spaces that he lorded over. This was the place where Tristam had grown up? I thought. A pang of sympathy shot through me, which I squashed ruthlessly. No doubt his gilded childhood had been filled with fancy balls and friends and foreign dignitaries. He didn't deserve me to feel sorry for him.

It was strange walking through the wide empty corridors as if we owned the place, not needing to sneak or hide. I held my breath and kept my footfalls soft as we padded past two guards in the purple and gold livery that I had come to recognize as belonging to the house of Obanstone and the realm of Faerwild. The king's symbol—a clenched gloved fist (subtle, that)—was emblazoned in gold gilt across the doors we passed and stained into the leaded glass of the windows. It seemed to be some of the only décor he'd seen to.

As we continued to walk, I started to realize that getting out unseen wasn't the hard part here. It was figuring how the hell to get out in the first place. The palace was a maze. We passed a few servants here and there hurrying quietly, or pairs of guards flanking doorways, but we couldn't exactly stop to ask any of them for directions. We could hardly even whisper to each other for fear of being overheard. So we threaded our fingers together and walked silently, hoping that the next turn would be the one that would lead us to freedom.

We turned down a long hallway that seemed promising —at the end of it stood two tall, broad wooden doors crossed with iron bars. A servant turned from a side hall directly in front of us—a lovely faerie female with jet-black hair and arching eyebrows.

Orin's grip on my hand tightened painfully, and he let out an audible gasp.

The faerie woman froze where she stood, looking around, her pointed ears trained for the origin of the sound.

What happened next was inexplicable. Orin pulled his mask off, revealing himself to the woman.

"What the hell—" I started, but my panicked whisper was cut off by one wavering word.

"Mother?"

Holy shit! This was Orin's mom?

The look on her face confirmed it. Her dark eyes went from shock to delight to motherly worry in the span of an instant. "Orin," she cried. She looked around surreptitiously before hurrying towards us and grabbing Orin's arm, pulling him back into the side hallway she'd come from. "What are you doing out of your room?" she asked.

"That's all you have to say to me?" he asked, hurt playing across his handsome features.

"Of course not," she said, pulling him into a tight embrace and burying her face into his chest.

He wrapped his arms around her, and I looked away, feeling as if I was intruding upon a very important moment. A minute later, I realized the futility of my action. I still had my mask on. They couldn't see me anyway.

"I've missed you so much," she said. "Your father and I have been following the race closely. We're so proud of how far you've come."

"It's all for you. If I win the boon, I'm going to free you both."

"Oh, Orin." She pulled back. "You know we'd never ask you to put yourself in danger for us."

"You didn't," he said. "You didn't have to. How are you? Are you all right?"

She nodded slowly, and I thought I recognized the mask that fell over her features, schooling them into indifference. She didn't want Orin to know how things really were here. "We're fine. It's not ideal, but we make the best of it. At least your father and I are together. We had hoped we would run across you while you stayed here, but we feared to reach out directly. The king is very strict, and his instructions were clear. The staff was not to have any contact with the contestants."

"Why?" Orin asked.

She shook her head. "He's very paranoid. I think...It's not important. Where are you going?" She changed the subject.

"We're going..." he hesitated. "Jacq, come here. Take your mask off and meet my mother, Ramona."

I pulled my mask off hastily. "Hello, Mrs. Treebaum," I

said nervously. I couldn't believe I was meeting Orin's mother. I felt so unprepared. I hadn't dated many guys, but usually, parents liked me. This time, I wasn't so sure. What did she think about her son being with a human? Though... the camera hadn't caught our kiss, so she couldn't know we were anything other than teammates. Maybe that was for the best. No need to add potential prejudices related to interspecies dating to the list of complexities we were dealing with today.

"It's so nice to meet you, Jacqueline. Thank you so much for looking out for Orin."

"Looking out for me?" Orin scoffed. "If it wasn't for me, Jacq would run into danger any chance she got."

"You take care of each other," Ramona said. "You make a good team. It's clear to anyone who's watching that you're the strongest team."

That was nice to hear. We hadn't been able to see any of the dynamics of the other teams, other than the short time we'd been partnered with them in the Elemental Trial. And then we were all on our guard. It was crazy to think that the public, who had nothing to do with the race, knew more about parts of it than we did.

"Orin, it's dangerous for you to be out here, out of your room. The king's instructions were clear." It seemed she couldn't miss an opportunity to mother him. It was kind of sweet, really. "And why the masks? The invisibility?"

"We're going to see Jacq's sister," Orin said. He looked at me with a questioning glance, and though I appreciated it, I nodded. I didn't think Orin's mom was going to spill the beans about Cass. "We think there is something going on. With the race, and a group called the Brotherhood of the Rose and Thistle. We think Jacq's sister has something to do with it, but we're not exactly sure."

"The Brotherhood?" Ramona's dark eyes widened.

"You know of them?" I asked, eagerly.

"Oh, yes. It's not common knowledge, but if you pay attention, you see signs of their work here in the palace. The king is deeply involved in the group. There have been humans visiting here for the past few months, involved in clandestine meetings. Shipments of things that are squirreled away under the utmost secrecy."

"Faerwild and Earth used to be joined together. We think the Brotherhood is trying to merge both realms again," I offered our theory. "Do you think the king would support something like that?"

"Expanding his power over millions of more souls? Humans, who are helpless against magic and could be controlled and potentially used for his purposes? Yes, I think that's something Vale Obanstone would be extremely interested in. Your father—" She froze as the sound of heels clicking on marble reached all of our ears at the same time. "Hide!" she hissed, and Orin and I fumbled with our masks, tying them back on. Just in time, for around the corner, spun the Faerie King himself. With none other than Patricia at his side.

"Ah, Ramona. I've been looking for you. We have need of your magic."

My hand fumbled for Orin's invisible one, and I found it at his side, balled into a fist.

"Of course, Your Majesty," Orin's beautiful mother curtseyed. Anger lit inside of me at the thought of this beautiful sweet woman being enslaved to that asshole for one-hundred years.

Patricia gave a fake smile and spun on her stiletto, with Ramona following after the odd pair like a faithful hound. I felt Orin move to follow, and it was all I could do to keep hold of his hand as he moved, towed along in his wake. I couldn't do anything without risking exposing us to the king, not hold Orin back or hiss at him to stop. All I could do was follow helplessly as we slipped through a set of double doors before the king closed us all in together.

3

———

My heart rate rose rapidly, not from fear of being caught, although that was a very definite risk, but panic that we'd be trapped here, unable to reach Cass on time. It's not as if we were locked in here, but the chances that a phantom door opening would pass unawares was next to nil.

I recognized the room we were in immediately. It was much quieter than I remembered with only the five of us in here, but there was no doubt in my mind that this was the room they'd brought us to at the end of the first trial. The room where they'd made us look presentable before parading us in front of the general public. I guess we had been in the Faerie palace, after all.

One of the mirrors was still there, and it was here where Patricia now stood, gazing at herself with a frown.

"Come here now," she barked, and for a second, I wondered who she was talking to.

As Ramona hurried up beside her, Orin's hand squeezed mine tighter still. At this rate, it was going to fall off due to restricted blood flow. I shook it a little and Orin lessened his grip.

"My boobs aren't perky enough," Patricia snapped, lifting them an inch or so. It was such a weird comment. Why did anyone care about her chest? "I want to look like a twenty-five-year-old...no...an eighteen-year-old."

I almost gave us away by snickering. She might have remarkably wrinkle-free skin for her age, but there was no way she could pass for twenty-five, let alone eighteen.

"And make them bigger," she continued. "Just a touch. I don't want to look like a ridiculous blow-up doll."

"Yes, ma'am," Ramona replied. She closed her eyes and took a deep breath. Although I couldn't hear her speak, her lips were moving as though she was uttering an incantation. As I watched, a purple surge of light surrounded Patricia. Her chest lifted slightly and swelled out, pressing against her suit jacket and making the buttons strain.

The glow faded, and Ramona's eyes fluttered open, but Patricia was gazing only at herself. She was grinning like a cat, slyly and full of admiration of her new perky breasts.

So, she was fake. Well, that was hardly a revelation, but the extent of her fakeness was astounding. Makeup and plastic surgery weren't enough anymore. She was resorting to magic to maintain her appearance. And the way she was so comfortable here as if this was all so familiar...how long had the Faerie king been indulging her desire for magical alteration?

"Bravo." The king clapped his hands and gave Patricia a matching Cheshire cat grin, making me want to puke. In that moment, he reminded me something fierce of his son, Tristam.

"Make me thinner too." Patricia turned to the king and

returned his smile. "You feed me too well, Vale. I feel like a whale."

"Nonsense, nonsense. You have the figure of a supermodel." What was this? The general meeting of the Patricia appreciation society? Seriously, when had these two become so chummy?

"True. I'd still like to lose a few inches." She patted her flat stomach and looked sternly at Orin's mother.

Ramona, once again, raised her hands and concentrated them on Patricia's stomach, which shrunk to almost comically tiny proportions. If Barbie had grown up, this is what she'd look like.

"My hair." Patricia turned to the king. "Vale, do you think I went too blonde before?" So Ramona *had* performed this service for Patricia before.

"You look perfect as you are, Patricia." He walked over to Patricia and kissed her cheek, causing her to giggle like a schoolgirl.

"I think it should be a shade lighter. Did you know I came in second in a Hollywood's sexiest presenter's poll last year? I think with your help and your slave, I could make first place."

Beside me, Orin gripped my hand tighter again, and I could understand why. Patricia was as disgusting as Vale Obanstone. He treated people like shit, and Patricia was no better. God, they deserved each other. Is this what Orin's mom had to put up with on a daily basis?

"You." Patricia snapped at Ramona, even though she was less than three feet away and could hear perfectly well. "Make me blonder, and I want my hair longer."

"As you wish," Ramona gave a respectful little bow and then performed a spell that turned Patricia's hair almost white. I grinned. I was just thinking, if it were me in Ramona's place, I'd be itching for a little revenge.

"Not that blonde," screeched Patricia. "I look like an old hag with grey hair. Think Marilyn Monroe, not granny chic."

Ramona's eyebrows knotted together at the command. She probably had no idea who Marilyn Monroe was.

"Do it, slave," the king added, not even looking towards Ramona. It was like he was speaking to a pet. "Do you not hear her?"

Ramona nodded then redid the spell; this time, giving Patricia a head of gorgeous pale gold locks.

Orin's hand pulled against mine, and I reached out with my other hand and grabbed his wrist, holding him tight. I had no idea what he was thinking, but judging by the direction he was pulling, he was headed towards his mother or would be if I let him. I took it as my cue to get us out of here. If we didn't leave soon, Cass would wonder where we were, or worse still, would leave without us. This might be my only chance to see her. Plus, if he was trying to get to his mother, we'd end up caught, and I'd never get to see Cass.

I jerked on Orin's hand, but he remained steadfastly pulling in the opposite direction. I yanked harder, urging him to move, but he wouldn't budge. I could understand why he didn't want to leave his mother with Patricia and the king, but there was nothing we could do to help her. Not right now. Behind us, a door opened. I used the distraction to whisper in Orin's ear. "Leave her. She's a strong woman. She'll be fine."

Checking behind me, I saw the servant had left the door open. This was our chance.

Thankfully, Orin listened to me and surrendered in our game of invisible tug of war.

We ran to the door and slid through quietly.

My mind was buzzing as we hurried towards the two huge wooden doors. There were so many things I wanted to say to Orin. I wanted to remind him that getting through this godforsaken race was the best way to help his mother. I wanted to scold him to keep his eyes on the prize like he'd done for me so many times over the last two trials. But most of all, I just wanted to thank him for coming with me when he so badly wanted to stay with his mother. But I couldn't say any of those things for fear of being overheard. I could only hope he knew how grateful I felt.

Two guards flanked the wide doors, which were shut tight. We slowed to a stop a few yards from them, and I chewed my lip, wondering what the hell we were going to do now.

But something miraculous seemed to happen. First, one guard, then the other, started to nod off, their handsome faces dipping towards their chests. Soon, one let out a burst of a snore, the other swaying on his feet.

"Come on," came Orin's hushed whisper. We tiptoed past them holding our breath, and Orin pulled one of the huge doors open. It creaked on its hinges ominously, and we froze, but neither guard woke. We shut it silently behind us.

I blew out a shaky breath as Orin took my hand again, and we hurried down the wide stone steps in the front of the palace.

The main gate was flanked by guards, but the tall ornate wrought iron panels were wide open. A bolt of excitement shot through me. We were free in Elfame, nothing but a few city blocks between Cass and me. Free of monsters, free of games, and most importantly, free of Vale Obanstone. No cameras, no Patricia, no guards, or FFR staff. I was practically giddy with the power of the realization. Out here, it was just Orin and me and the night.

4

———

"This way," Orin spoke, making me jump. I'd gotten used to the silence, but it wasn't needed out here. Out here we could say whatever we wanted.

I pulled my mask from my face, ruffling my blonde hair. I wanted to spread my arms wide and spin in circles, *Sound of Music* style.

"Put that back on," the disembodied voice of Orin said. "We're famous here. Everyone knows who we are. We can't risk getting caught before we find your sister."

Damn. He was right. I had forgotten. Fame was a real hassle. I pulled the mask back over my face, and we set off into the night.

But at least, we could talk now. "I'm sorry we had to leave your mom," I said as we crossed a wide thoroughfare. Maybe it was good I had my mask on because I could gawk without feeling out of place. This was my first real glimpse of Elfame, and I couldn't believe what I was seeing.

It was like a movie. There were no cars here, no technology. It was late, so the streets were quiet, but I still spotted faeries in all shapes and sizes moving around us—down the street, up in the windows of nearby manor houses, backlit by the purple glow of magical lighting. From what Orin said, King Obanstone's palace compound sprawled across the northwest end of town, and we were heading southeast towards a more commercial area.

I heard Orin's heavy sigh. "I'm glad you did. I was about two seconds away from punching the king of the Seelie Courts, and I can safely say that I'd have been eliminated from the race if I had. You did me a favor."

"One more trial, and then it's over. We only have one more team to defeat. Then you can free her. We're so close."

"I know. I just...it was hard seeing it firsthand...how they treat her. It was easier to imagine that she lived a simple life under the king's radar. But her magic is unique, and...I was fooling myself."

"What does her magic do? Just manipulate appearances?"

"All faeries have the ability to create glamours, to cast a spell to make something look different than it actually is. But my mother is half elemental, so her connection to the earth and living things makes her able to make those glamours real. To actually manipulate how a person looks. I inherited a little of the gift from her, but she's much more skilled than I."

"So, you could make my boobs, like, as perky as an eighteen-year old's?" I asked in a valley-girl voice, imitating Patricia.

"Your boobs are perfect as they are," Orin responded, and I was glad I was invisible so he couldn't see the scarlet flush creeping up my cheeks.

"Thanks," I managed. "Did it seem like Patricia and the king were really frickin' cozy?" I whispered, searching for a safe subject that was not my boobs. I craned my head as we passed an incredibly tall faerie that looked like a praying mantis with stick bug legs.

"Yes," Orin said. "It was clearly not the first time they did that."

"We know Patricia's involved with the Brotherhood. And your mother thinks the king is too. Maybe they knew each other before the race."

"Maybe…" Orin was quiet, and I took that moment to take in some more of the sights around me. Tall light posts carved to look like trees held purple lights in their iron branches, illuminating our path. We passed a green park with a broad circular fountain where tiny fish jumped in and out of the water, their silver bodies glittering like stars. The houses we passed were huge and fancy, with ornate gates and tall white columns and sweeping lawns. Damn, these faeries lived the good life.

I was jerked backward by the tether of Orin's hand as he stopped cold. "What?" I asked as I got my footing back under me. "We need to hurry."

He started moving again. "Sorry, I just realized something." His voice sounded strained.

"What?"

"What if Patricia and the king *did* know each other before the race. Through the Brotherhood. What if the race was *planned* by the Brotherhood? What if this is all a front for their mission?"

Now it was my turn to stop short. "To merge the two realms?"

Orin tugged me forward. "Come on, we are already cutting it close." He was right. We didn't have long; that was for sure.

I stumbled along, my mind spinning, moving the disparate pieces that hadn't seemed to fit together. They still weren't quite meshing. "I don't get why they'd want to hold the race. What does it have to do with their goal of combining Earth and Faerwild? I would think the publicity would be bad news for their evil schemes."

"I don't understand it either. I just...it never really made sense to me why after centuries of isolation, the king suddenly decided to expose Faerwild to the humans in such a public way."

We reached a corner and stopped, letting a glittering carriage pulled by two black horses trot past. A faerie riding some sort of sinuous lizard passed by the other way, and I let out a little gasp of disbelief.

"It's just one more block up and then a few blocks to the left," Orin said. "The Goddess of the Moon is a well-known theater. I'm assuming they picked it because they knew I would have heard of it."

We hurried across the street, back under the canopy of trees lining the street. "Do all faeries live like this? If this is what Earth was being merged with, I don't know if it would be so bad..."

"No way," Orin scoffed. "This is the equivalent of, I don't know, the richest part of the human world."

"Beverly Hills?" I offered.

"Sure. The area surrounding the palace is prime real estate. The poorer faeries live on the outskirts of the south end of the city in teetering buildings filled with tiny tenements and flats. A couple of families crowded into one room sometimes. It's hard to find work, hard to find food."

I furrowed my brow. "Can't faeries just magic up everything they need?"

"No. There are strict laws about what you can and can't use magic for. And most faeries can't just create from nothing. It's easy to go hungry in Elfame."

"But, you conjured that sleeping bag back in the Sorcery Trial…"

"I didn't create it, I summoned it. I had purchased some supplies I thought I might need, and back up supplies for good measure. I just used magic to transport it to where I was in the race."

"And you couldn't have summoned us some pancakes?"

Orin let out a little laugh. "I didn't realize we'd be so short on food. I hadn't prepared for that. And I couldn't summon it from someone else, it would be stealing. I could go to prison, especially for doing it so publicly."

I contemplated that. I'd been so fixed on getting through the race, that I hadn't really thought much about faerie society or Orin's life.

"Why don't more faeries just live in the wild, off the land?" I asked.

"Why don't humans?" he countered. "You saw it out there. Some do. But it's dangerous and lonely, and a hard life. Most faeries would rather try to make their living in cities and towns, just like humans."

"Where do you live?" I asked.

"I live with some friends on the outskirts of Elfame. But if I win that million dollars, I'll buy my own place."

"Did you have a job?"

"I'm a security guard for a richer fae family. But I was hoping to go to school. Learn a trade, like my father."

Huh. Orin's life sounded a lot like mine, in a weird way. Shit job, shit apartment, struggling to make it amongst a million other faceless people trying to make it. Maybe we had more in common than I'd ever realized. "You do have the security guy death glare down pat," I offered. "I bet you're good at your job."

"The security guy death glare?" Orin asked.

"I remember the first time I saw you. You were in your leather jacket, dressed in all black, and when you looked at me, it was like you were trying to shoot laser beams at me with your eyes."

"Funny, that's not how I remember that going. I remember spotting you and thinking that no human had the right to look so beautiful."

Orin's words stunned me, and I swore I felt my heart physically swoon in my chest. I was definitely tongue-tied searching for the appropriate reply. Thankfully, I was spared finding one when Orin went on to say: "Then you saved that stupid girl in the audition and schemed your way into the race, and I knew you were going to be trouble."

"I did not scheme my way into the race!" I said indignantly, but my words trailed off as we turned the corner onto a wide square that displayed a stunning marble structure lit from below by purple faerie lights.

"The Goddess of the Moon," Orin said softly.

We hurried across the square towards the theater's soaring steps and spires, the mosaic flagstones beneath our feet forming a geometric pattern. I pulled my mask off eagerly, baring me to the quiet night. Orin followed suit. We slowed to a stop just shy of the steps.

"What now?" I asked. I looked around. Was it past midnight? Had we missed her? The square was totally deserted.

Or so I thought. A moment later, strong hands grabbed me from behind, and a black hood was thrown over my head.

5

I kicked out behind me, hoping to find purchase against my attacker. At the very least, I wanted to break a bone or cause some damage, but they were way too quick and much too skilled at what they were doing.

"Orin!" I shouted, hoping he would hear me and shout back, but all I heard was the rustle of the cloth over my ears and the thick voice of my abductor telling me to be quiet. Like hell, I was going to be quiet. We were in a city. Sure, it was midnight, but some people were around, and if they could hear me, there was a chance I'd be rescued.

I opened my mouth to scream, but before I let it out, a large hand clamped down over it. Moving my head quickly, I maneuvered my mouth and clamped my teeth around the perpetrator's fingers, biting down as hard as I could.

"Shit!" I heard him cry out. "She's a feisty one!"

A woman's voice mumbled something back to him. The sack around my ears muffled the sound, distorting her words so I couldn't make them out.

I was thrown into what felt like a car, but we were in Elfame, so it was probably some weird faerie mode of transport. The doors slammed shut, and as we set off along the bumpy road, silence enveloped us.

"Jacq. Are you okay?" It was Orin. He'd obviously been thrown into the same conveyance I had. As my wrists had been tied behind my back, it was impossible to reach out to him, so instead, I moved my foot forward until I felt his shin.

"I'm fine. Listen. I think I can get out of this. I took classes."

"Hollywood has classes on how to escape kidnapping?"

"You bet your ass it does," I said, maneuvering myself into an upright position.

"And humans think faeries are strange," Orin huffed.

Ignoring him, I maneuvered myself into a position where I could work at the binds on my wrists. The rope they'd used was tied tightly but not expertly. These amateurs had never been Girl Scouts! I twisted my wrists, slowly loosening the knot. From there, it was a matter of time before I was able to loosen it enough to pull my hands free.

"I'm free!" I said as the car or whatever it was came to a halt. I pulled the sack from my head as the doors opened.

"And that, gentlemen, is why we failed to nab her at Hennington House."

I knew that voice. It took my eyes a few seconds to adjust to the light, but when I did, I saw Cass grinning at me from outside the open doors of the vehicle.

At the sight of her, my heart seized and my throat constricted, my lungs twisting so tight I couldn't breathe. "Cass?" I whispered, barely able to get the word out.

Beside me, Orin, with the hood still over his head, echoed my word in the form of a question. "Cass? Your sister, Cass?"

"The one and only. Come on. Let's get you two out of

there." Cass held out her hand to me as two guys pulled Orin out and retrieved the hood from his head. It was her. Really her. Her blonde hair was cut short and curled around her chin in a bob, and her face was thinner, more serious than I remembered it—though she was still just as beautiful. She wore dark jeans and boots and a black tank that showed off her toned arms. So much about her was unfamiliar and new, but then she grinned at me with her crooked smile, and it was all Cass.

I couldn't hold back the tears as I leapt into my sister's embrace. I held onto her, fearful that if I let go, I'd never see her again. I was aware of movement around us, but I couldn't see anything through the cascade of tears that flowed down over my cheeks.

"Damnit, Jacqueline, I promised myself I wouldn't cry, and now you've got me going!"

"Duckface," I said, referring to the childhood moniker I used to torment her when I was feeling like an especially evil little sister.

"Monkeybutt," she retorted.

I laughed so hard, I snorted. It was like we'd never been apart.

"Peabrain."

"As amusing as this all is, can someone let me know what's going on?" I turned to see Orin gazing at the pair of us as though we were lunatics. For some reason, it made me laugh more.

"Sorry, Orin. I'm being rude." Cass untangled herself from me and walked over to him, her hand outstretched.

It gave me time to look at exactly where we were. The roughly hewn walls gave me flashbacks of the mine in the first part of the Elemental Trial, but this was no mine. It was a bunker of sorts. Behind us trailed a sloping tunnel, which

I assumed we'd driven down. The car we'd come in looked almost like a car made on Earth but without the polished finish. It was rusting and old and had no hint of its former color. Huh. I didn't know they had cars in Faerwild. It must be magicked somehow.

"Come on, let's get inside," Cass said. She strode forward and twisted a large metal handle to open the iron door before us. She seemed to be running this operation, or at least in charge of the two others with her.

One was very obviously fae, with pointed ears peeking out from under his curling golden-blond hair. I knew exactly who he was. He was the faerie that I'd seen Cass with all those years ago. This male had been front and center in my nightmares for over two years, but now as he stood smiling at me, I found he wasn't threatening at all. He was handsome with too long floppy hair and a disarming smile that ended in dimples. He reminded me a little of Tristam. Pushing that rat to the back of my mind, I turned my attention to the other guy. He was human, or at least, he appeared that way. Italian maybe, or Greek? He looked like a Wall Street trader in his grey suit and wingtip shoes. I didn't recognize him at all.

We stepped through a rusted door into a space lit by flickering faerie lights. Two threadbare sofas sat in the middle of the room, flanking a coffee table covered in rings where coffee had spilled, and no one had mopped it up. Apart from that, there was a huge desk shoved against the far wall that was covered in paperwork and a pile of books strewn in a messy heap. The ICCF logo was blazoned on a flag covering a large portion of the wall behind the desk. How was the International Coalition for Cooperation with Faeries, the international government organization that controlled faerie/human relations, involved in this?

"I'm Louis," the human said, moving forward to stretch out his hand. He'd caught me looking at him. "Sorry about the kidnapping. It was the safest way to do this. I really hope we didn't scare you."

"Scare Jacq?" scoffed Cass, turning and crossing her arms before her chest. "Haven't you been watching the race? This woman fought dragons for fuck's sake. Goblins! Hell, she even managed to get one past the Erl-King."

Louis smiled at me, apologetically. "Of course, I've been watching the race. You're quite the hero. Cass was a complete mess when you got trapped in the prison in Deep-hold. The Merfolk are brutal."

"I wasn't a mess," called out Cass, flinging something soft at him. Looking down, I saw that it was the sack that had covered Orin's head. "I knew Jacq would escape. She managed to get away from us at Hennington House, remember?"

My eyes widened. So it had been Cass who'd orches-trated my attempted kidnapping back before the Elemental Trial started? I'd fought my attacker off, thinking he or she was out to hurt me in some way or, at the very least, take me out of the race. If only she'd said something. Anything. If I'd have known it was her, I wouldn't have fought. I'd have gone willingly wherever she wanted me to go. She was the reason I was in the race in the first place. I never needed the million dollar prize. It was all for Cass.

The faerie male stepped up beside Louis, and though I'd hated him for years, I found felt strangely comfortable in his presence. He hadn't kidnapped Cass. I knew that now. She'd come here of her own free will. Years of resentment fell away as he offered up his hand to me. "And I'm Auberon," he said, taking my hand in his.

"Dragon's balls," Orin cried out. "You're Auberon Oban-stone. I knew it!"

Auberon Obanstone? As in Vale and Tristam Oban-stone...as in the heir to the faerie throne?

"Wait, what?" I stammered, looking from Auberon to Orin who appeared even more confused than I was. "I thought you were dead?"

Cass came to my side. "We have so much to tell you. Come and sit down. Auberon, honey, can you conjure up some coffee for these two. I think they're going to need it."

Cass took my arm and guided me to one of two sofas that were the only soft furnishings in the whole room. It didn't escape my notice that Cass had just asked the crown prince of Faerwild to make us coffee. And he was doing it too. Well, he was making it appear out of thin air which was nearly the same.

As he handed a cup to me, I struggled to get over the fact that this was Tristam's brother. They did look similar—with the same dimples and the exact same shade of hair, but I couldn't, for a second, imagine Tristam making the effort to get anyone coffee.

"Thank you," I said shyly. Now that I knew who he was, coupled with the thoughts I'd had about him over the past few years, I found myself nervous and at a loss for words. Cass sat next to me with a cup of tea. I'd forgotten that she hated coffee. What else had I forgotten about her?

Auberon sat on her other side, and Orin and Louis took seats on the other sofa. It was all very cozy.

"It's time you got the whole story," Cass said. "Let's start at the beginning..."

6

Cass took a sip of her tea and then began. "A long time ago, Earth and Faerwild were the same realm."

"Before the magicians split it," I nodded. "Right, we read about it in *A Disunion of Worlds*."

Cass raised an eyebrow at me and exchanged a glance with Auberon that I think said, *See, I told you she was smart and totally ahead of the curve.* Or at least, that's how I decided to interpret it. "You already know?"

"Well, sort of. We know about the Brotherhood and how they want to rejoin the realms. We suspect Patricia and the king are Brotherhood. What we don't know is what the hell it has to do with the race. Or you. Or us."

"Maybe I can chime in here and fill in some gaps," Auberon said. "A few years ago, I started getting suspicious about some of my father's business dealings. He was acting strange and secretive, smuggling humans over the Hedge for meetings that I knew weren't approved by the ICCF. I started snooping. I learned about the existence of the Brotherhood—those were the humans he was covertly meeting with—Brotherhood magicians. I learned what they wanted to do. Merge the human and faerie realms once again, so magic could return to the Earth, and my father could rule over all of it."

"Because Auberon isn't a psychopath like his father, this alarmed him greatly," Cass said. "As you could imagine."

"But I was young and arrogant. I thought I could convince my father that what he was doing was wrong. I confronted him about it, and he locked me in my room. I think he was trying to figure out what to do with me. I was the crown prince of Faerwild, after all. But, I knew I needed to tell someone what he was planning. My father is the most powerful male in Faerwild, but there are powerful leaders on Earth, too. I decided to go over the Hedge to see if I could find the authorities and tell them what he was planning. I stole a few of the books that contained some of the history, a map of his plan, and snuck out of the palace."

Auberon looked down like it was hard for him to keep talking. Cass patted his knee. I guess it would be hard, leaving everything you knew to betray your father and keep him from ruining the world.

Cass picked up the story. "Auberon came through a portal in central Montana. He walked for days, sticking to the forests and back roads, stealing food, trying to avoid humans. He was near exhaustion when he walked through our backyard, practically running into me."

"Cass was a fierce little thing." Auberon regarded her with an adoring look in his eye that twisted my heart. "She wrapped me in bonds of air, freezing me to the spot, and demanded to know what I was doing there. I was so shocked to find someone doing magic, and so beyond the point of exhaustion, I just started laughing."

"And then crying," Cass said, a grin on her face. "He was

just laughing, with tears streaming down his face, and he asked if I had anything to eat. He said he'd like something to eat before I killed him.' So, of course, I had to help him."

"Where did you hide him?" I asked. I couldn't believe all of this was going on and Cass hadn't told me!

"Gen's family had an old hunting cabin that they didn't use very often. He stayed up there, and the coven and I fed him and let him rest. Once he was feeling better, he started telling us why he was there. He showed us the books, and the girls and I decided we would help get him to the ICCF."

"There was an ICCF facility in Seattle, and we reached out to them by phone. Once they got over thinking we were prank callers, they agreed to meet us mid-way to take me into protective custody," Auberon said. "At that point, Cass and I had already started to fall for each other and didn't want to be apart. But, I convinced her to stay and finish school."

Cass turned to me. "That night, when I told you I was going to be gone for a few days, I was just going to drive Auberon to meet the ICCF agents, and come home."

"You could have told me," I said softly.

"I should have, but I figured the fewer people who knew, the better. And no offense, but you've never been a great liar. I was afraid you'd spill the beans to mom and dad that I was keeping a faerie in Gen's hunting cabin."

Fair point. "So, what happened? Why didn't you come home?"

"Plans changed," Auberon said. "We were gathering our belongings when the ICCF called and told us that several faeries had crossed the same circle I had, including one of my father's captains. The ICCF was tracking them, and they were headed straight towards us. Using magic, they had found out where I was and that I was staying with Cass."

Louis spoke next. "I was Auberon and Cass's ICCF contact. It was clear from our intel that the king knew of Auberon's location and Cass's involvement. For their safety, we moved them to a secure location, into our version of witness protection. The time we spent in Helena "investigating" your sister's disappearance was actually to ensure your family's safety, Jacq."

I rubbed my face, trying to take it all in. Faerie conspiracies? International witness protection? It all sounded like the stuff of Bond movies.

"It's nice of the ICCF to get involved," Orin said carefully, "but why? Aren't you just a bureaucratic organization that approves visas and stuff? How do you even have the capacity to do something like witness protection?"

"You two read through *A Disunion of Worlds*, right?" Louis asked. We nodded. "So you know that an international group of kings and magicians worked together to separate the worlds. That alliance has never gone away— it still exists to keep the human and fae worlds apart and to protect us from each other, if necessary. It has had many names and faces over the years—the ICCF is just the most recent."

"Wait, hold up," I said. "The ICCF is an ancient magical organization?"

Louis nodded.

This was getting stranger and stranger. I turned back to Cass. "You're in witness protection. What I don't get is why you couldn't write to us. At least secretly! We thought you were dead!"

"And it killed me to have to go dark Jacq; trust me, it did. I wanted to reach out covertly a thousand times, to drop hints I was alive. But it was too dangerous. The ICCF couldn't be sure that the king wasn't watching you. He didn't take Auberon's disappearance lightly. I couldn't put you guys in danger by reaching out."

That made sense, I guessed. But it still fucking sucked. Everything we'd been through...all that grief and pain and anger...it all felt so pointless now. She had been fine. She had been safe. My throat started to tighten, and I could feel the tears coming. I couldn't give in to them, not right now. We still didn't understand what the heck was going on.

Orin, blessedly, moved us to the next topic. "So, what does this have to do with the race? With us?"

"The original magicians who split the human and faerie realms set up a magical wall of sorts, between the worlds," Auberon said. "The Hedge. It's anchored into the fabric of reality at five points. These points are marked by powerful magical spells attached to the earth by physical monoliths. Both the physical and magical elements are necessary to keep the wall intact. If the physical and magical halves of each of the five anchors are compromised together, the wall will fail, and the two realms will be merged together once again."

"So that's what the king is trying to do?" I guessed. "And his Brotherhood buddies?"

Louis, Cass, and Auberon nodded together.

"The ICCF carefully monitors everything and everyone that passes over the Hedge," Cass said. "To destroy all the anchors, the Brotherhood needed weapons and magicians to power them. We think the race was a ploy to distract everyone, to allow new faces and technology into Faerwild. It would be much easier to sneak in a MED and a magician to power it among all the camera equipment and studio staff than to do it on a quiet portal that the ICCF is watching carefully."

"MED, as in, magical explosive device?" Orin asked.

Auberon nodded. "Besides, my father is an egomaniac. It would play into his ego to have his triumphant destruction of the Hedge broadcast for both worlds to see. At least, before all technology went dark for good."

Suddenly, things started to become clear. The weird metal detector and magical screening we'd had to go through before we started each of the trials. The ICCF was searching for these devices.

"If you know the king and the Brotherhood are planning on blowing up the anchors, why don't you just arrest him?" I asked.

"We have jurisdiction in Faerwild at the king's discretion only," Louis said. "He's cooperating with us, but he doesn't have to. It'd be like the U.S. trying to arrest the president of another country. Pretty hard to do. So our primary objective is to prevent the Brotherhood from destroying the Hedge. If we can publicly expose the king's plan, turning public sentiment in Faerwild against him, Auberon would have a chance to regain the throne and then he'd have the power to punish him accordingly. That's our ultimate objective."

Damn. This was complicated.

"Gen was our girl on the inside," Cass said. "She worked for us and was trying to discover the location of the final anchor."

"So, *that's* why the king sabotaged her ring." My eyes grew wide. "Cass, I'm so sorry."

Cass's face was grim. "Thanks. The Brotherhood has been on us through this whole operation. They raided our main headquarters in Elfame, and we barely made it out. Gen knew there was a risk that she'd be exposed, and she went in willingly."

"Doesn't make it any easier to lose a friend, though," Auberon said, rubbing Cass's back gently.

"No, it doesn't." She shook her head.

Everyone was silent for a moment.

"You don't know where all the anchors are located, then?" Orin asked quietly. "If that's what Gen went in to do."

Auberon stood and walked to the desk, retrieving a wrinkled piece of parchment. "According to the old records that the ICCF keeps, there was only one rendering of the locations of the anchors. The magicians who created the Hedge didn't want the anchors to be easily located. Somehow, my father had gotten his hands on it. When I left the palace, I stole it, but I didn't realize the map was so old, the bottom had torn off. We only know the location of four of the anchors."

He knelt down between the couches, placing the weathered scrap of paper on the coffee table. Orin and I leaned in, inspecting its ancient, faint writing. I tried to orient myself, to look for any landmarks I recognized. Not that I was a geography whiz, but I had tramped across some of Faerwild by this point. "Ohmygod. Is that Emerald Mountain?" I asked, pointing at a little peak depicted on the map.

Cass nodded. "We think so."

I looked up. "I saw some crates there when we were fighting the dragon. I forgot about it until now. They had the rose and thistle on the side."

Cass and Auberon exchanged a glance. "That confirms our suspicions. They're getting everything into place to blow the anchors."

"Is this the Sylph palace?" Orin asked.

"We think that some of the checkpoints for the various trials have been strategically located at the anchor points, so the Brotherhood can place their explosives there without suspicion," Auberon explained.

"How many anchor points have they gotten to?" I asked,

my heart speeding up in my chest. How close was the Brotherhood to making their twisted plan a reality?

"We think four," Louis said. "The final trial will take place here in Elfame. Which makes sense, because we think the final anchor is located somewhere in the city. But we don't know where."

I sat up, my eyes wide. "If they manage to place the final charges and get their magician in place at the last checkpoint, then when we get to the end of the race, to the final checkpoint..."

"Boom," Cass said, spreading her fingers wide. "Life as we know it ceases to exist."

7

Silence rained down on us. It was such a bold statement. Terrifying even. *Life as we know it ceases to exist.*

"What exactly does that mean?" asked Orin. "It's not like everybody would die, right?"

Cass shook her head quickly. "Nothing that dramatic. But the Earth of the twenty-first century—the world we know, it'll all be gone. Faerie magic interferes with electricity. To sustain technology like the cameras used by the FFR takes complicated spells that require constant maintenance. If the Hedge comes down, there will be no cars or internet or air-conditioning or credit cards.... it'll all be gone. It will be like going back to the dark ages. Can you imagine the chaos as humans try and adapt to living that way again?"

I leaned forward, trying to take it all in. "What can the king possibly have to gain by plunging us all into darkness?"

"I think I can answer that," Auberon chipped in. "In a word, power. My father's the king of Faerwild, but that isn't enough for him. He's always hated that humans, without the aid of magic, have managed to build cities and amazing technologies. In comparison, Faerwild looks like a backward little village. There are billions of humans on Earth, but only seven or eight hundred thousand faeries in Faerwild. He wants to conquer the humans so he can rule over them. The easiest way to do that is to take away the one thing that all humans rely on. Technology."

"I told you he was a psychopath," butted in Cass. "That's why we need to stop him. We were hoping you and Orin would go back into the race and help us look for the last anchor point. We need someone who can get close enough to see what the king and his lackeys are doing. You two are really our only hope."

I looked over at Orin. He was shaking his head. "I don't know. I don't want the Hedge to fall, but for me, this was always about winning. Getting the boon and freeing my parents. I need to focus on that."

"I think your parents would want you to help," Auberon said. "I think they would believe the greater good is more important than two faeries."

Orin looked up, his dark eyes blazing. "How the hell would you know? You don't know them."

"Actually," Louis said gently. "We do. We have certain sources on the inside, feeding us information. Your father is one of them."

Shock froze Orin's features.

"Is that true?" I asked Cass, who nodded.

"They've been instrumental in getting us information about the race and the other Brotherhood members. For instance, we believe there's a Brotherhood member among the race staff."

"Patricia," I said.

"You knew?" Auberon said.

I nodded. "She's not very subtle with all her rose and thistle jewelry. I guess once I knew there was something to look for, the signs were obvious. I think Niall, one of the original coaches, worked for the Brotherhood too. He started to provide me information before the first trial, but I think he got in trouble for it because he was kicked off the staff the very next day."

"Will you consider what we're asking?" Louis said. "Even if you could find the remaining piece of the map, that would be hugely helpful."

I bit my lip, considering. I wanted to help, but I didn't want to speak for Orin. We were a team—and something more. I didn't want to force him to do anything.

So he surprised me when he stood up, his hands balling into fists. "I'll do it. Someone has to bring him down. I'm glad it's going to be me. I want to see the look on his face when he falls."

There were no prizes for guessing whom he was talking about. "It won't be just you bringing him down," I stood up too. "I'm going to help too."

"And we'll have your back," Cass said.

"That's right," Auberon added. "You won't be alone in there. You'll have our support."

"And the full support of the ICCF," Louis said.

So just like that, an agreement formed between our strange group. Two sisters from Montana, one human dressed like a bank manager, and two faeries, one of which had stolen my heart and the other who was the son of the king we were trying to bring down.

I knew that we couldn't stay here forever; we had to sneak back into the palace before dawn. But I needed some time alone with Cass. It had been so long, and we had so much to catch up on. We drifted to the far side of the bunker, facing each other. Part of me still couldn't believe she was really here. She asked about our parents, I asked about her life in Faerwild. We talked and talked, falling into the comfortable pattern we'd had when we were young.

"I nearly died when I saw Peaches on TV," Cass said, talking about the raggedy doll my mind had conjured up in the Sorcery Trial. "I thought it was a trick or something to make me come out of hiding. And when Orin swiped me with that sword. Auberon had to talk me down from the ceiling I was so scared. It all felt so personal."

I thought back to that part in the first trial. It had been personal. The magic of the mirror had taken our memories and twisted them into something grotesque. No wonder Cass had freaked when she'd watched it.

"It's time to go," Auberon said, hours later. "Orin is nearly falling asleep on the sofa, and you two have a job to do in the morning....well, later this morning. It's nearly 4 a.m."

"Huh? What job?" I asked stifling a yawn.

"The third trial starts in about five hours." Auberon reminded me.

Crap. In my happiness of seeing Cass again, I'd forgotten about the race and the madness that surrounded us all.

I didn't want to leave. I'd spent the last few years doing everything in my power to get to this point. To find her. Cass must have seen my reluctance because she hugged me tightly and whispered in my ear. "We'll all be together when this is over. I'll finally be free and able to come home." It was the jolt I needed.

"We'll be together again soon." I nodded.

She passed something to me that looked like an old-fashioned hand-held mirror, in a little round compact. She passed an identical one to Orin.

"In case I need to powder my nose?" he said around a yawn.

"To communicate with us," she said. "If you want me, call my name into the mirror. Don't do it in front of anyone else and make sure there are no cameras on you. Hide in a sleeping bag or something so they don't see you."

I nodded at her instructions. It didn't feel like nearly enough, but knowing I would be able to speak to her whenever I wanted helped soothe the burning ache in my chest.

Auberon passed me the magic mask that had fallen off at some point en route and escorted me to the strange car. This time Orin and I sat up front with Louis who was driving.

Auberon and Cass stayed behind.

Out of the back window, I watched her waving at me, slowly disappearing from view as we sped up the tunnel and out into the city.

It was quiet at this time of day, and we barely saw anyone as we drove. Louis pulled up a few blocks from the palace, where we could get out beyond the sight of the guards. "Good luck in the next trial," he said to us as we got out.

"Feel free to help us cheat at any point," I said with forced cheer. The thought of the impending trial hung over me like a cloud.

He laughed. "We'll see what we can do."

Getting back into the palace was easy, as doors were being opened and shut for early morning deliveries. We silently padded back to Orin's room without event.

I flopped into bed, my eyes aching with lack of sleep. As

I felt Orin's arms gently pull me towards him, I fell into a peaceful slumber.

Seconds later, someone knocked urgently upon the door. At least, it felt like seconds, but as the sun was now streaming in through the windows, there was a good chance a few hours had passed.

I practically fell out of bed.

Opening the door, I found a squat woman with short-cropped bright red hair and a nose ring.

"Hello?" I bleated, trying to keep the surprise out of my tone. I had no clue who she was, but she looked as out of place as you could get in Faerwild.

"Still in bed, were ye?" The older woman snapped in a thick Scottish accent, surprising me even more. "There'll be none o' tha' nonsense while I'm with ye."

My brain obviously hadn't had nearly enough sleep because I couldn't understand a word she said. I turned her words over in my mind and attempted to translate. She'll have none of that nonsense while she is with me. With me? Why would she be with me anywhere?

"I'm sorry. Who are you?"

"Tha name's Ruth. I'm ye new camerawoman. The king asked me to come an' git ye."

My mind stuttered. Oh. So she was Ben's replacement. It had to happen, but it didn't mean I had to like it. Thoughts of easy-going Ben flashed through my mind, and the pieces of my heart seemed to crumble further. Poor, sweet Ben, with his blood spilling out onto the white sand. He was irreplaceable. He hadn't even been dead twenty-four hours. It felt wrong to have anyone take his place. It felt wrong to even continue to the next trial. This whole damn thing was wrong, wrong, wrong.

All I could manage was, "We're coming," before I closed the door in her face.

I turned and sagged against the door. "It's time to go," I said to Orin, my voice flat. A heavy weariness washed over me that had nothing to do with my lack of sleep.

God, I hated this trial already, and it hadn't even started yet.

8

We followed Ruth to a ballroom where a spread of food had been laid out for us. There were only two round tables in the cavernous room, one of which was filled by Tristam and Sophia and their camerawoman. I piled a generous helping of eggs and bacon and fruit onto my plate, doing my best to ignore them. Ruth was humming before me as if she didn't realize that her predecessor had been brutally murdered by faeries just one day before. Maybe she didn't know. I wouldn't put it past the FFR to leave that little nugget of information out of the job description.

We sat down and dug in. Orin leaned over, nodding his head towards where Tristam and Sophia sat. "It's strange, isn't it," he said. "That it's down to us four."

I nodded. "I think part of me never believed we'd make it this far."

"Me too. In another few days, this could all be over." His words struck me sideways. He was right, but there was one part of this race that I didn't want to be over, not at all. And that was spending my days with Orin. I put my fork down, my stomach churning.

He seemed to know what I was thinking. No doubt he'd thought of it himself. "We'll figure it out," he said, putting a hand on my knee. "I promise."

But would we? There was no way in hell I'd want to live in Faerwild, and would he want to live on Earth? Away from his parents, from everything he'd ever known? It was notoriously difficult to get a permanent visa for a faerie to live on Earth...though I supposed the ICCF would totally owe us if we helped them save the world and all. I tried to imagine walking down Sunset Boulevard with Orin, hand in hand. Going to the beach...cooking dinner together in an apartment. It was so hard to picture those domestic scenes when all we'd ever known was danger and adrenaline. What if we didn't even like each other when things were normal? Safe?

"I said we'll figure it out," he said again, shaking my knee. I met his eyes. "But later. For now, we have to stay focused."

I nodded and bit down on my bacon, chewing mechanically.

Patricia breezed into the room in a shirtdress of olive green with tan leather booties, and to my surprise, she pulled up a chair next to me. I tried not to look at her boobs, imagining how they'd been magically enhanced just hours ago. I focused instead on the two white envelopes in her hand. "I just wanted to extend my condolences for the passing of Ben, your cameraman," she said. "It was a tragedy, and there will be a full investigation."

"Really?" I leaned back, surprised. She almost sounded sincere.

"We take safety very seriously at FFR," she said, nodding.

I grimaced, crossing my arms over my chest. Now I knew she was full of shit. But she pushed to her feet and walked to the middle of the room, signaling one of the cameras. I guess her little apology was over. "Contestants, it's time to receive your final clue and start the next trial, the Master Trial. This race will take place right here in Elfame."

We all stood, forming into a little semi-circle around her to get our instructions. There was a distinct gap between the two teams. Oh yeah, it was on.

"At different times, and in different ways, the last two trials tested your magic, your knowledge, your logic, your strength, and endurance. This final, Master Trial will test all those and more. It is down to just two teams. At the end of this trial, two of you will be millionaires." Patricia paused for dramatic effect. "I hold in my hand a clue for each of you. You will be dropped at different locations in the city. Don't open your envelope until the race begins." She handed Sophia and me the envelopes in dramatic fashion. And then the cameras went dim. I hurried back to my plate to grab my last piece of bacon, and we were off.

I had gotten my first glimpse of Elfame last night, but no one was supposed to know that, so I did my best to look amazed as we sat in a carriage that carried us away from the palace.

We crossed bridges and large plazas, and the city began to change, morphing from the bright white marble of the palace to dingy brick and stone.

"This is the old town," Orin said as we passed through an opening between what looked like two old stone walls. "The original Elfame. It was contained within these walls. Now it's in the center of town, surrounded by the rest of the city that built up around it."

"Tha king has cleaned oot tha ol' town," Ruth said,

waving her hand out the window.

"The whole thing?" Orin goggled. "There must be thousands of homes in here. I can't believe people would agree to it."

"Reckon he dinna give 'em much choice."

Our carriage ground to a halt outside a large rectangular building of red stone. "End of the line," our driver called down. "Head inside."

The three of us got out of the carriage, and I realized how strange it felt to be separated from the other contestants. This was different—starting out alone. Somehow, it felt more final. Orin pulled open the large wooden door painted with black lacquer, and we ducked into the low light of the building.

It was a large warehouse, empty but for a few ratty couches and a battered table. High windows leaked light through their dingy faces. Strangely enough, the floor beneath our feet was painted bright white. Why would someone go to the trouble of sprucing up the floor, while leaving everything else dusty and worn?

"I hope we don't have to stay here for long," I said, surveying the warehouse with distaste. Though, at least for the moment, the space seemed safe.

"Read the clue," Orin suggested.

I ripped open the envelope and retrieved the piece of cardstock inside. "It's a poem. Or a riddle." I read it aloud.

It's time to prove your mastery,
   Of color and piece and square,
   One at a time you'll find them,
   Those you love so fair.
   But if you are to end it,

You mustn't take the bait,
Across the board you'll soldier,
'Till king becomes your mate.

"WHAT THE FUCK DOES THAT MEAN?" I asked when I'd finished reading.

Orin shook his head. "Damned if I know."

"We have to make friends with the Faerie king?" I ventured a guess. "Or find him? If this is another trial tailored for Tristam, I'm going to scream."

Orin scowled. "And I'll join you. But, the king's at the palace. Do we just need to get back to there?"

"It seems too simple." I shrugged. "What's this other stuff? Those you love so fair? Taking the bait?"

"I suspect we'll find out."

"So, best we can figure, we head back to the palace?" I asked.

"Until we know more...that's my best guess," Orin agreed.

"Feels like a bit of a letdown."

"Just wait until the monsters start popping out." Orin opened the door and gestured for me to go first.

I stepped out onto the sidewalk and looked around. It was quiet here. Too quiet. A breeze ruffled a nearby tree, making me jump. I was seriously on edge.

"The sidewalk is painted white," Orin said. He frowned and looked back over his shoulder into the shadow of the building. "Like the interior."

"Weird," I said and started walking. The sooner we got done with this trial, the better.

We walked down the sidewalk in the general direction of the palace. Its tall white spires were visible from nearly everywhere in Elfame, so getting there was just a matter of pointing ourselves in that direction and walking.

I was about to step off the sidewalk to cross a vacant street when Orin threw out an arm to block me. "Wait."

I froze and looked around quickly. The street was deserted. "What?"

He pointed. "The street is painted black. Look at the dividing line here."

I looked down beneath my boots. He was right. While we stood on the white sidewalk, the street and the sidewalk on the other side were painted black. "Do you think it's like, hot lava?" I joked weakly.

"What?" Orin furrowed his brow. "Why would you think that? It looks cool and stable to me—"

"Never mind," I said. "It's a kid's game."

He shot me a look like, *what crazy kind of kid were you*, but he knelt down tentatively to poke the black-painted street. His finger hit what I could only describe as a...force field.

"Woah," I said, and Orin stood quickly, stepping back. "Are you okay?"

"Yes, it was unpleasant, but not painful," he said. He reached out a hand slowly and pressed it against the air. A violet field appeared around his hand, undulating in the air.

What in god's name...

Orin grimaced and pressed harder, trying to shove the field back. Nothing. He couldn't budge it.

"What the hell is going on?" I asked, looking down at the riddle in my hand. There was something we were missing here.

But another voice answered—not Orin's, and not Ruth's. It was low and scratchy and came from directly behind us. "Maybe I can answer that."

9

———

I whirled around, readying myself for danger, but the voice turned out to belong to a squat creature with green-tinged skin, pointed ears, and a flat nose. While he was small and didn't appear to be threatening, I kept my guard up, not trusting the appearance of anything in this hellhole.

"It's a leprechaun," Orin whispered in my ear. "Attracted to gold, wily as a cat and completely insane."

"I can hear you," the creature sang, doing a set of surprisingly acrobatic cartwheels around us. "And I'm not completely insane, only partially. Plus, we're the only ones on this street, so I'm all you've got."

I shook my head, trying to take everything in. I thought leprechauns were traditionally meant to be lucky? Something told me that wasn't the case with this guy. He pulled three live mice from his pockets and began to juggle them. "So, do you want to get through the barrier or not?"

"Yes, please," I replied. I didn't particularly like the idea of needing help, but if he could get us closer to the palace, I'd take what he had to offer.

"No," Orin grabbed my hand and pulled me back from the leprechaun. He lowered his voice, turning to me. "Have you learned nothing about this race? No one in here is our friend, and no one wants to help us. We'd be better off figuring this out ourselves."

"I can still hear you," The leprechaun shouted at us, but his tone wasn't hostile. It was almost...gleeful. "And I'll be your friend if you want me to. My name's Peachkin. Would either of you like a mouse?"

Ignoring him, I turned back to Orin. "I agree, but unless you know how to get through this force field, we're stuck here. At least, following him might get us a little closer to where we need to be. He doesn't seem dangerous. He's too busy juggling mice for a start." I snorted in laughter, a grin creeping over my face at the absurdity of it all. That grin was short-lived, however,—as I looked back at the leprechaun— er, Peachkin—I caught him eating one of the mice while juggling the other two with one hand. Blood dripped down his chin as he chewed on the mouse.

Bile rose in my throat at the sight of it. Poor little mouse.

"What was it you were saying?" Orin asked, batting his impossibly long eyelashes at me.

I huffed. Damn it, I really needed to get out of this place.

"Don't you at least want to see what I can do?" Peachkin asked. He scurried between Orin and I, up to the line where the road turned from white to black. He held his finger up in the air. The other two mice had been stashed in his pocket, presumably for a snack later.

"Come on, let's find another way to go," Orin said, taking my hand, but I was rooted to the spot, grossly fascinated by the strange little faerie. What was he waiting for?

The leprechaun cocked his head to the side, and as he

did, a distant sound filled the air. It sounded like... a resounding gong.

Peachkin did a little jig on the spot and jumped across onto the black side of the street.

"I guess we can pass now," I said, following the leprechaun. Orin trailed reluctantly after as I held my hand out over the line where the magical field had been. I waited for the shock or whatever it was that had stopped Orin, but nothing came. Taking a deep breath, I stepped forward onto the black-painted street.

"It's fine." I turned back to Orin.

Reluctantly he followed my lead and passed through without incident.

"That way?" I asked, pointing down the street. Ramshackle houses and shops flanked the black-painted cobblestone thoroughfare. As I took in the sinister street, a sense of foreboding hit me so strongly that I almost expected scary music to start blaring out at us like in a horror movie. But the peaks of the palace turrets could be seen over the top of the houses, and this appeared to be the natural path. There was nowhere to go but forwards. Besides, if I froze every time I got the heebie-jeebies in this place, I'd never go anywhere.

We walked the street for a mile or so before it once again turned white beneath our feet. At the border between black and white, I expected there to be another magical field like the last border, but we passed through with no resistance.

I gripped Orin's hand as we walked cautiously down the street. Everything was so dark and still, even with the white paint on the cobblestones. We passed rows of abandoned shops. A grocery store, a spell bookshop, a toyshop. Had the king cleared all of this out, just for the race? Peachkin skipped next to us, whistling a merry tune. I still didn't trust the little guy, but he seemed to know something about what was going on. So I was okay letting him accompany us. For now.

All of it put me on edge. The silence and shadows of our surroundings juxtaposed with the merry little flesh-eating leprechaun. I was glad when we reached the end of the street, and once again, the world became black. As I stepped across the line where white turned to black, my foot bumped up against a purple haze, and an invisible wall of magic pushed me back.

"Ow," I complained, my toes smarting.

"You can't go yet," Peachkin said gleefully. "It's not your turn." He pulled a flute out from his other pocket and began to play a tune while tap dancing on the spot.

"Not our turn?" Orin growled at the leprechaun in frustration. "What does that even mean?"

Peachkin shrugged his little shoulders and gave Orin a grin.

My eyes widened as the clues began to click into place. Not our turn...We were playing a game.

"Orin," I exclaimed, grabbing his shoulders. "Give me the clue again."

He fished it out of his jacket pocket and handed it to me.

I scanned the clue, testing the language against my hypothesis. Piece and square...board...king...Holy crap!

IT's time to prove your mastery,
   Of color and piece and square,
   One at a time you'll find them,
   Those you love so fair.
   But if you are to end it,
   You mustn't take the bait,

*Across the board you'll soldier,
'Till king becomes your mate.*

I LOOKED UP AT ORIN, shocked. "It's chess. We're in a game of chess. Look at this." I turned the clue to him. "The old city has been turned into the gameboard. White and black squares. We don't need to befriend the Faerie king, we need to beat him! Checkmate!"

Peachkin clapped his hands together in glee then carried on his playful tune.

Orin nodded slowly. "You're right, Jacq."

"We can't move until Tristam and Sophia have taken their turn. They need to figure out what they're doing, too."

"I never learned to play chess. I know there are multiple playing pieces."

Pride and excitement flooded me. Finally, a trial I'd be good at. A trial that I'd know what the hell I was doing. I knew chess. I'd played hundreds of games with my father when I was younger. "I know how to play. The most common pieces are the pawns. The pawns can move one space forwards except at the start when they can move two if they wish. To be able to take an opponent, they can only do it diagonally and then only by moving one space."

Orin shook his head. "Are we pawns then? Who are the other playing pieces? If we're looking for the king, surely there have to be two to make this a fair game?"

I bit my lip. "Yeah. So maybe it's not the Faerie king after all. But then, who is it we're supposed to find?"

"I don't know. Maybe it has to do with these lines of the clue: *Those you love so fair? Not taking the bait?*"

"Maybe," I admitted.

He was asking so many questions, questions that I didn't

know the answer to yet. I knew this was chess, I just didn't know how it was being played out in real life. If we were waiting for Tristam and Sophia to figure it out and make their move, we were probably in for a long wait.

"I saw a toy shop a few stores back. Let's see if there are any chess sets in there, and I'll give you a crash course."

Orin looked like he'd rather do anything than walk back down the street, but he relented. Really, he had little choice because we couldn't pass through the barrier to the white square yet. This trial was about cunning and patience, and we both had to learn that particular skill.

The toy store was marked by a hanging sign with gold lettering. Expecting it to be locked, I tentatively tried the handle. Surprisingly, it opened easily. The shop smelled musty and had a fine layer of dust on the floor, but footsteps in the dust told me that someone had been here recently. I followed the trail of prints. They led to the games section. Whoever had come in here had walked out again because the same prints led back out to the door.

This was nothing like any toyshop I'd ever been in on Earth. It was as dark as the street outside with macabre objects on each shelf. The only source of light coming from an aisle a few rows away. The doll section creeped me out as we passed. They looked more likely to murder someone with their red eyes than comfort a little child. "If you all grew up with toys like this, I'm not surprised the fae are so bizarre and deadly," I said, picking up a particularly worrying doll with a dark green body and terrifying face.

"This isn't a toy shop," Orin said with horror. "This is a DM toy shop. Strictly adults only. And give me that doll. Some of the magic in shops like this is seriously messed up. Look at the label." He grabbed the doll from my hands like it was a ticking time bomb and put it back on the shelf.

I leaned in to read the label. *Tibetan Head Shrinking doll. Hold this for more than ten minutes, and your head will shrink to a quarter of its size. Perfect for enemies.*

I swallowed hard.

"In fact, don't touch anything," said Orin. "Half the objects in here could accidentally kill you. Or curse you."

I moved to the center of the aisle to be as far from the shelves as possible so as to not accidentally shrink my head or worse. "DM Toys?" I asked. It sounded like some sort of kinky faerie sex shop.

"Dark Magic. The faeries that frequent this shop are not the kind you want to meet in a dark alley." I declined to point out that category included almost any kind of faerie at all. Orin continued, "I'm sure some of the stuff gets used for harmless pranks, but I'd be willing to bet that the customers of a place like this are thieves, murderers, and vagabonds. Let's find what we came for and get out of here quickly."

I wasn't sure I wanted to find a chess set now. If a doll could shrink my head, what could an evil magical chess set do? But then I saw one on the shelf and changed my mind.

"I think we were supposed to find this," I said, approaching cautiously. The set was at least twice the size of a normal chess set to account for the layout of the city. A dome of glass covered it, and it was here that we found the source of the blue light that lit up the dreary shop. I wondered if the FFR producers had purposely placed it in our path. Would we have found it somewhere else if we hadn't stumbled in here?

The playing pieces were formed of glowing magic, and it didn't take long to find my and Orin's likenesses standing on a black square near the edge of the board. Flicking my eyes to the other side, I saw Tristam and Sophia, just one square from the start. Had they figured out what was going on yet, or had they just stumbled across? Either way, we were in the lead. I was filled with a sense of glee that was completely unjustified. We'd literally only moved two squares after all, and chess could be a long game. Still, it was nice to know we were beating Tristam and Sophia.

Orin grabbed my hand and pointed to the board. "The king isn't *the* king. Look."

I moved my eyes to where he was pointing—the square where our team's king should be. A handsome man wearing a crown stood on the square. I didn't recognize him, but I brought my hand to my mouth as I saw who the queen next to him was.

"That's my mom," I cried in a strangled voice.

"And our king is my father," replied Orin. "The FFR has gotten our family involved!" His hands balled into fists. "We aren't playing a game, Jacq. This is a war."

10

———

I fought against my rising panic. "She must be so terrified!" I said, peering at the little piece. It was motionless, its little face a still mask. The pieces must just mark locations the board, not reflect what was going on with the actual human or faerie players. "We have to go to her!"

"But we can't leave our square," Orin said as we passed out of the toyshop back into the dark street.

Peachkin was doing a handstand in the middle of the street.

I looked back down at the chessboard, which I was holding before me like a tray of hors d'oeuvres. "Peachkin," I called out to the leprechaun. "Are you one of our pawns?"

He righted himself and giggled gleefully. "Right-o!"

I guess we were stuck with him.

"Can you shrink this thing?" I asked Orin as I struggled to balance the chessboard.

Orin nodded and waved his hand. Purple magic swirled around it, and the chessboard shrunk to the size of a book. Much better.

"Peachkin, how can we get to the queen's square?" I asked. "Peachkin!" I snapped my fingers. The little faerie was practicing his backflips, which by the look of it, he hadn't quite mastered. Ow.

"I can't go with you," was all he said.

I grimaced and turned back to the miniature board. "Do you think we're stuck on this square until it's our turn?" I asked Orin. He peered through the glass at the board.

"No, that doesn't make sense. How would we move the other pieces then?"

"But, we tried to cross, and it didn't let us until the gong sounded." I assumed the gong was Sophia and Tristam's turn running out, but they hadn't realized they needed to move. So this was timed, like a professional chess game. That made it even more challenging. But it made sense that the race producers would want to keep things moving.

"We were here, right?" Orin pointed at a white square on the board. "We moved Peachkin here, up two. Maybe we can't move into the center of the board without moving one of our pieces. But what if we tried to go back the other way, to these squares that hold our other pieces? Maybe we can move that way."

I shrugged. "It's as good a theory as any. I don't see how we'd be able to move them without at least speaking to them. Let's check it out." I glanced down the street a few yards to where Ruth was standing against a building unobtrusively, filming us. I turned my head so she couldn't see what I was saying, and whispered. "How the hell are we going to find the last anchor point if we can't even move from these stupid squares?"

"I don't know," Orin said under his breath. "One problem at a time." Orin took the board from me and tucked it under his arm.

I turned to the leprechaun. "Peachkin, we're going to visit our other pieces now. We'll see you later, right? You have to stay here?"

"Peachkin will be here in wait, my lady." the leprechaun flourished an impressive little bow, and I had to fight the smile on my face. The weird little guy was kinda growing on me, mice-eating aside.

We turned back the way we came, jogging through the black-painted streets towards the white square. When we came to the boundary, I held my breath, bracing for the purple border to halt our progress, but we passed through with ease. Relief welled in me. "Maybe it allows us to pass back through the squares we've already traveled through."

"That would make sense."

We walked side by side, me striding as fast as I could without jogging, Orin, peering at the gameboard. "Jacq, our other pieces...you'll never believe who they are."

"Who?"

"Molly, Duncan, and Niall."

"What?" I ground to a halt, peering into the chessboard. He was right. The little figures were unmistakable. I'd been so focused after seeing my mother that I hadn't even looked. I hadn't seen Duncan since his and Yael's unfortunate run-in with the red caps during the Sorcery Trial.

"Molly is one of our rooks, Duncan is one of our knights, and Niall is our nearest bishop," I said, surveying their positions on the board. It seemed that somehow, there were two of each of them on the board. I couldn't even begin to understand how that kind of magic would work. Our pawns appeared to be eight little Peachkins.

Now I was more confused than ever. "Do you think they agreed to be a part of this voluntarily?" But then why the hell was my mom here? My mom had a certain toughness—

she faced double-black-diamond ski runs and a mother moose passing through our backyard without blinking—but taking a dangerous trip to Faerwild didn't seem like her style.

"I don't think my dad would have agreed. But it's hard for me to imagine the other racers could be compelled to participate, let alone Niall. We need to talk to them," Orin said. We redoubled our pace, breaking into a run.

Niall was as much of a mystery as my mom. A Brotherhood member was one of our pieces? But Niall had always seemed like a bit of a loose cannon—he tried to help me, then he got booted off the race staff, and then he and Patricia had been arguing. Was it possible that he was on the outs with the Brotherhood? That he could be a resource for us? But if he wasn't...what did that mean? Was the king onto us? The Brotherhood? They'd already sabotaged our rings...perhaps suspecting my connection with my sister. Now that we were really working for the ICCF, was it possible they'd placed Niall to undermine or expose us?

The thoughts spun in my head like wild tops, and in the end, I shoved them all aside. I needed more information to figure this out. And there was only one way to get it. Keep moving.

We neared the edge of the white square and slowed to a walk. "This is one of our pawn squares," Orin said, looking at the gameboard. "We should be able to cross." We both braced ourselves as we stepped across, but we passed over the division without event. I blew out a breath. "Okay. Now we know. We're free to move among the squares holding our own pieces."

It was easy to make our way to my mother now, just a matter of crossing the squares bearing our pawns and then cutting over to the queen's square. I could tell Orin wanted to go to his father, but he silently conceded that my mom was the priority. She was a human in an unfamiliar city. Orin's father could wait.

We came to a halt in front of a columned three-story building that declared itself as the Elfame Library. "This is the main building in this square. I'll bet she's in here," Orin said. It was all I needed.

I ran through the front doors, taking in the huge antechamber cradled by dual staircases and a crystal chandelier.

"Mom?" I cried, my voice echoing in the cavernous space. "Helen?" I'd pounded up the steps to the second-floor balcony when she appeared before me. In the flesh. My mom.

I crashed into her, wrapping my arms around her in a stranglehold. "Holy hell, mom," I said into her short blonde hair. "Are you okay?"

She sighed into me, her arms squeezing me just as tightly. "It's so good to see you, darling," she said, as we rocked back and forth. I couldn't believe she was here. As much as I wanted her as far from Faerwild and the FFR as possible, I couldn't deny how comforting it was to have her here.

A cleared throat sounded behind us, and I remembered Orin. I untangled myself from my mom's arms and turned to Orin. "Orin, this is my mom, Helen Cunningham."

"Hello, Mrs. Cunningham," Orin said, his hands in his pockets, his head ducking. I'd never seen him look so contrite!

My mom opened her arms and closed the distance between them. "We Cunninghams are huggers, Orin. It's so nice to finally meet you."

I held back happy tears as my mom embraced my faerie

boyfriend. Ha! That was something I'd never in a million years have predicted. Her mention of us Cunninghams made me think of Cass. I desperately wanted to tell her that Cass was alive—that I'd seen her—but I couldn't with Ruth filming everything. Damn cameras. I supposed a few more days of ignorance wouldn't hurt, as much as I longed to spill the good news.

They broke off the hug, and my mom patted Orin's arm. "Thank you for taking such good care of Jacqueline."

"It's my pleasure," Orin said, rather than the normal snarky comment I expected about how I always ran into danger. I guess Orin was determined to be on his best behavior.

I inspected my mom surreptitiously. She looked none the worse for wear—she was wearing boots, jeans, and an FFR zip jacket. Her short hair was fluffed in its usual style, and she wore just a hint of makeup—mascara and lip gloss. She didn't look like a woman who had been stolen out of her home by faerie operatives.

"Mom, how are you here?" I asked. "This is crazy! Are you okay? Did anyone hurt you?"

"Oh no," she said, her hand flying to her chest. "The race staff have been wonderful. They told us they wanted to do something dramatic for the final trial and asked if we'd be willing to help out. They promised we'd be perfectly safe."

I pressed my lips together, fighting the dread that lanced through me. They'd promised Ben he would be perfectly safe too, and look where that had gotten him. But I couldn't tell her that. I didn't want to scare her. She was in it now. We'd have to finish it. To keep her safe.

"So they didn't...force you to be here? Against your will?"

"Oh, no, of course not!" My mom seemed shocked by the very idea. "I admit I was a little ambivalent about the idea of coming here, but I'm not going to let myself be frightened of something just because it's new or different."

Orin must have been thinking the same thing I was because he spoke carefully. "I know they promised to keep you safe, but there have been things in the race that even the FFR producers didn't foresee. Just...be careful, okay? For your sake and Jacq's."

Mom nodded. "Of course. I'm taking everything seriously. But I couldn't pass up a chance to see you, honey. And I want to help. Is it my turn to move somewhere on the board?"

"Um, not sure," I said. The gong hadn't sounded, indicating Tristam and Sophia's turn was up. But maybe it wouldn't if they had moved.

Orin was examining the little chessboard. "Yes!" he looked up. "It's our turn. Time for our next move."

11

———

I grabbed my mother's hand, but before I'd even moved one step, she pulled me back.

My heart plummeted when I realized why. Taking my mother with us meant putting our queen into play. She was the most important piece on the board and taking her out this room too soon would be a colossal mistake. It was possible as Peachkin had moved out of one of the spaces diagonal to her, giving her a free path, but I wasn't prepared to lose her in any sense of the word.

"Where did they move?" I asked, trying to figure out if there was any possible way to move her with us without jeopardizing the game. I already knew the answer. Of course, she couldn't come with us. Maybe it was possible to play a whole game of chess with only a queen, but it was way beyond my skill level.

"They moved a pawn two spaces forward," Orin answered. "It's diagonal from Peachybum or whatever he's called. Does that mean we can take him?"

I checked the board over his shoulder, finding it hard to care. I didn't want to leave this square, not without my mom.

"Theoretically, we can take their pawn, but it leaves Peachkin open to attack."

"So where do we move?" he asked, peering down at the board, his face screwed up in concentration. I gave him a crash course on chess, pointing out which pieces could move where.

"See here...This guy on a horse is a knight," I said, pointing at one of Tristam and Sophia's pieces.

"Ario, you mean."

Peering closer I saw the little figure had wings. It was, indeed, Ario. They must have had their top faerie healers work on him if he was ready for action again this soon after the Elemental Trial. I thought he and Molly had resigned? I wondered how much they promised to pay him to get him back here. No doubt, the producers thought it would be that much more compelling to make us fight our old rivals. I fought the urge to slam my fist into his little playing piece and tried to concentrate on the game.

"Knights can move one to the front, back, left or right," I explained, "and then two squares along making an L shape."

"I can't see a problem with us taking their pawn," he said. "I can't see where anyone would attack us."

I shook my head and examined the board again. "You can't go in all guns blazing in a game of chess. You have to think two or three moves ahead and try to anticipate the other team's move. It's a tactical game. Maybe Peachkin will be safe now, but we have to ask ourselves why the other team basically sacrificed one of their pawns on the first move."

"Jacq," he said, pulling the gameboard away from me. "You'd be right if we were talking about a normal game of chess. When you're cozy in front of the fire playing games with your father, I'd say you know the best way to play, but remember, this is also the Fantastic Faerie Race. We can anticipate the hell out of it, but the truth is, no matter what we do, the FFR will screw us over somehow. We need to move, and to do that, we need to leave here. Your mom is safe for now. Let's not get bogged down in the intricacies of the game. We need to move forward. For all we know, Tristam and Sophia don't know how to play and are just blundering along."

I nodded, knowing he was right. The timer was ticking down too, and if we didn't move soon, our turn would be lost. I'd memorized the positions of the pieces on the board. I could plan as we walked.

I gave my mom one last hug, swallowing the secret she, above any other, should know. That Cass was alive and well, not more than a few miles from here. But I couldn't tell her. Even uttering my sister's name would cause some reaction, be it good or bad. I had to be content in the knowledge that Cass would be able to see her on TV.

"Bye, Mom. Please be careful."

"I wasn't allowed to say much, but they promised me a nice cup of tea when you leave. Now get out there and kick some faerie ass. Present company excluded, of course," she added, turning to Orin and hugging him too.

I hated to leave her on her own, but she seemed safe, and I had to remind myself we were on TV. Knowing my mother, by the time this was all over, she'd be running her own chat show and writing her memoirs: *The time I had a cup of tea on the Fantastic Faerie Race, by Helen Cunningham.*

Finding Peachkin was pretty simple. He was exactly where we'd left him, but now, he was riding a unicycle and playing a harmonica.

"Peachkin," I called.

He turned and gave me a merry little wave with his free

hand. "Howdy doodly o'ho," he answered back after taking the harmonica from his mouth.

"We need you to move one square northeast."

Peachkin pulled a compass from his waistcoat pocket and studied it. "Northeast, you say? We'll be taking another piece?"

Orin nodded. "Another pawn like yourself."

"Yippee!" Peachkin hopped down from his unicycle, which vanished into thin air. Then he started a little jig.

As quickly as the unicycle disappeared, new items magically materialized around Peachkin—battle armor on his body and a long sword in his hand. "Let's do this!" he sang and charged off ahead of us.

Orin looked over at me and shrugged.

We pelted off down the street to catch up with him. For a fellow with such short legs, he sure was fast. At the end of the street, he turned left until we were right at the very corner of the white square. He hopped through the magical field as if it wasn't there and carried on his way. Orin went through after him, and I brought up the rear, trying to get a glimpse of the black squares at either side.

Peachkin was already way ahead of us, so Orin and I redoubled our pace to keep up with him. At the speed he was going, the little man could compete in the Olympic Games. When we finally caught up with him at a crossroads that I estimated to be in the very center of the square, both my chest and Orin's were heaving with the effort.

Peachkin was already locked in battle with another leprechaun, who for some inexplicable reason, was dressed as a pirate. The leprechaun in black bore a curving sword which he swung in wild arcs while Peachkin ducked and rolled out of the way. Wow, they were both pretty good.

I gripped Orin's arm as the two tiny folks fought, my

heart racing in my chest. Even though Peachkin was annoying and more than a little weird, that didn't mean I wanted to see him get a sword to his chest. "Should we help him?" I asked Orin, gnawing on my lip. The pirate pawn knocked Peachkin's sword out of his hand, and our pawn had to scramble across the ground to snatch it back up.

"I don't know if we're allowed to," Orin said. "What did the clue say? *Don't take the bait*?"

I hated to think it, but Orin might be right. It took all of my self-restraint to hold myself back, to stop from running in to help.

But it turned out, Peachkin didn't need it. The little leprechaun spun out of the way of a particularly vicious swipe, and then with a cry, ran at the other leprechaun, his sword outstretched, ready to come down on the other leprechaun's head.

I closed my eyes and cringed against Orin when a shock wave seemed to pass through me, followed by the chime of a bell. I opened my eyes to see a wave of purple around the opposing party's pawn shimmering and undulating. He was protected by some sort of shield! But, Peachkin's blow must have "won" the bout, because a shower of purple confetti was raining down around him.

The two little men bowed down to each other and then did a complicated double jig before the other guy turned and walked away.

"What just happened?" I asked, waving my hand in front of me to clear some stray confetti.

"We won the battle," answered Peachkin while he jumped up and down trying to catch as much of the confetti as he could.

I let out a surprised laugh. That was it? In my head, I'd expected carnage, but instead, we were treated to a little highland dancing and a ticker tape parade. Maybe the FFR execs were going easy on us this round, and it really was just a game of skill.

The gong sounded somewhere in the distance. Out there, Tristam and Sophia would be planning their next move. Despite Orin's thoughts that they might not know how to play chess, there was no doubt in my mind that Tristam would. His father wouldn't have come up with a trial that didn't give Tristam at least some advantage.

The gong sounded out again pretty quickly. Looking at the gameboard, I saw that they'd moved one of their pawns forward. As far as I could tell, it didn't put Peachkin in danger, but it did open up space for their rook.

"Come on," Orin said, moving forward.

"Wait!" I called, picking up the gameboard and racing after him. "We can't just keep going forward. This is chess. We need to figure out where to go. One pawn won't do it alone."

But it was already too late. Orin, with Peachkin by his side, had already walked across to the next square—they'd made a move.

The black cobbled streets gave me a sense of foreboding as we ambled through. Peachkin was open to attack from two pawns and the knight. I crossed my fingers that the other team decided to ignore us and open up the gameboard further down. But before I'd had a chance to complete that thought, a black shadow loomed over us.

12

"Nice to see you again, Jacq." Ario grinned down at me from a horse with a coat as dark as night. With Ario's black wings outstretched, he could easily pass for Death himself. I gave an involuntary shiver as I addressed him. "I wish I could say the same about you."

I'd thought Ario was bad enough, but Tristam stepped out of Ario's shadow, followed by Sophia, who tossed her glossy hair over one shoulder.

"Now, now, Jacqueline, play nice," Tristam said, smirking.

I flipped him the finger, not caring how this was all coming across on TV. If the viewers wanted to think I was an uncouth bitch, I was cool with that.

"We're here to fight your pawn," Ario said, spurring his mount forward so that it towered above Peachkin.

Peachkin retaliated by balling his hands into fists and waving them around in front of him in an almost comedic fashion.

I cringed at the size discrepancy between them, Ario sitting tall on the huge black horse and tiny Peachkin who was jumping up and down, excitement etched into his features.

At least, no one could die in this game, I thought as Ario materialized a sword from nowhere and pointed it at Peachkin. Taking a step back, I decided to watch the match rather than be a part of it. We couldn't win. It just wasn't possible. For one thing, they'd taken us, and this was now their square for this round, but most importantly, we couldn't win because a slightly deranged little leprechaun was no match for a powerful incubus.

I was resigned to our loss, but at the same time, hoped Peachkin could persuade Ario to do a jig with him once it was all over.

Peachkin let out a battle cry that was surprisingly fierce and charged at Ario's mount. The horse reared in alarm and Peachkin swiped with his sword, slashing the horse's side. The black beast screamed in outrage, and my mouth drew into a thin line. Low blow, Peachkin. It wasn't the horse's fault. It was one thing to pummel a pompous incubus, another to harm a helpless animal.

Ario struggled to get his mount under control as the horse danced back away from Peachkin's sharp little blade. In the end, he freed his feet from the stirrups and kinda rolled off the side, landing on the ground in an undignified heap.

I couldn't resist my snort of delight.

Ario pushed to his feet, a black look on his face. He clearly didn't like losing face on television. He retrieved his sword and surged forward, swinging the huge blade at Peachkin, who barely managed to get his own tiny sword up to parry. Ario's sword was as long as Peachkin was tall, and though the leprechaun was fast, Ario's reach and superior strength were sure to end it soon.

The two attackers were a strange sight—one tall and dark, his handsome face set in grim determination, the other small and green, yet with a merry smile on his face even as Ario slipped through Peachkin's guard, the tip of his blade slicing the leprechaun's arm.

I straightened and turned to Orin. "What the hell? Wasn't there supposed to be a magical shield? Like the other leprechaun?"

"I'm sure it'll kick in before a mortal blow. That was just a flesh wound," Orin said, but he didn't sound convinced.

Ario was like a shark, driven into a frenzy at the sight of blood. He hacked and swung at Peachkin with furious power, driving the leprechaun back until he stumbled, falling on his backside.

"Peachkin!" I cried as Ario stepped in to end the battle. He reared back and stabbed Peachkin right in the chest.

I recoiled with shock as green blood poured from the wound, as Peachkin groaned in pain. "What did you do?" I screamed at Ario as he stepped back, purple confetti bursting into the air around him.

Orin and I ran to Peachkin's side, batting away the cursed confetti. Fucking Faerie Race! Did they have no shame? A player was injured, and they were throwing confetti!

Orin cradled Peachkin's head as I took his hands. "Are you okay?" I asked, though it was clear he wasn't. His green-tinged skin was pale, making him look even stranger, and the mirthful glee had left his face, replaced with lines of pain.

"Can you heal him?" I asked Orin, trying to hold in some of Peachkin's blood. Flashbacks exploded through my mind like fireworks—Ben's red blood spilled on white sand—Orin and I trying to save him. My stomach roiled as I struggled to focus on Peachkin, to stay in the present. Why did this keep happening to us? To me?

Orin's eyes were closed, and his hands moved over Peachkin's wound. I knew he didn't have much skill with healing magic, but perhaps he could do something to keep the leprechaun alive until a medical team could get here. "He's slipping."

"Stay with us!" I cried, taking hold of Peachkin's little hand.

But his eyes were fluttering closed. "Was...an...honor," he gasped. Then his head slipped to the side, the life gone from him.

Orin and I stayed still for a moment, looking at each other with anguished hearts, Peachkin's body stretched out between us. Then Orin tenderly set Peachkin's head down on the cobblestones, and we both stood, turning to the other team. Wrath rose within me as I beheld Tristam, Sophia, and Ario, whose sword still dripped green blood.

"What. Did. You. Do!" I screamed at them, pointing my finger like a dagger. "The pieces are supposed to be shielded! This isn't supposed to be a battle to the death! This is a fucking reality TV show!" In some distant recess of my mind, I knew that I was coming completely unmoored. But I did not give a flying fuck.

To their credit, Ario, Tristam, and Sophia all looked shocked as hell. "I didn't think I would kill him!" Ario said, throwing the sword down. "I swear! We thought he'd be protected like our pawn was! I thought...I'd score what would have been a killing blow, and the round would be over! I'm not a murderer! Why the hell would I want to kill some little leprechaun?"

"I don't know, maybe because you're a psychopath! Like everyone else in this race!" I felt Orin try to grab one of my arms to restrain me, but I shoved him off before turning my rage on Tristam. "You did this. You and your father. This race has been rigged in your favor every step of the way! This is just another ploy by the mighty Obanstones!"

"Jacq, I swear, we didn't do this," Tristam said. "Why would I want innocent faeries to die?"

"You're lying," Orin said next to me, his voice low and deadly. "Every word that comes out of your mouth is a lie." He stepped menacingly towards Tristam, and it was my turn to grab for his arm. As furious as I was right now, this couldn't devolve into blows. We had bigger things to worry about. Like what the hell our next move would be. And what to do with Peachkin's body.

But when I glanced back at the leprechaun, his body had vanished. "Orin, look," I tugged on his sleeve. He glanced back, and uncertainty played across his face.

"See," Sophia said. "Maybe he wasn't even real. Maybe he was some sort of faerie...hologram spell."

I scoffed. "Ario, are you real? Do you feel like a holographic spell?" I strode forward and seized his sword from the ground where he'd dropped it. "Maybe I should stab you and see if you're nothing more than air."

The three of them shied back from me, Ario's hands flying up before him.

"Jesus, Jacq, quit with the drama," Sophia said, shaking her head.

I thought my head was going to explode. I swung the sword at her, pointing with the tip. "Oh, that is rich. *You* are calling *me dramatic*?"

"Okay, we're not going to accomplish anything here," Tristam said. "I'm telling you we didn't sabotage your shields. You don't believe me. That's fine. It doesn't change anything. The race goes on."

"It changes everything!" I cried. "For us, it changes everything! My mom is here, Tristam! Orin's dad!" Oh god. I hadn't fully realized before that moment what it meant. My mom was in real danger.

I thought I saw a flicker of sympathy cross Tristam's face. I chose to ignore it. "Just get the hell out of here."

Tristam and Sophia turned on their heel as Ario went back to retrieve his horse's reins. He hesitated.

"What do you want?" I barked at him. My voice was growing hoarse.

"Can I have my sword back?" he asked.

"No," I snapped. "I'm keeping it."

He pressed his lips together and gave a little nod before he turned and led his horse away.

Orin and I were quiet for a good moment before he turned to me. "I can't believe you kept his sword."

The ridiculousness of what I'd said washed over me, and I started to laugh, tears springing to my eyes.

"Come here," Orin said, pulling me into his arms. I let the sword drop with a clang, embracing him.

I sobbed into his shirt, balling my hands into fists in his shirt. "Poor Peachkin. He was such a little weirdo. He didn't deserve to die."

"No one does," Orin said, rubbing my back.

Except the royal Obanstones, I thought. But I kept the sentiment to myself, as I didn't think spouting treasonous sentiment on TV was a particularly good idea.

Finally, Orin released me, and I wiped my eyes.

"We need to get moving."

I nodded. "Orin...our parents. We can't play this chess game for keeps anymore. We need to protect our pieces. At all costs."

"I know," he said. "We'll figure it out."

"How?" I asked. "I don't know what to do."

Orin ran his hands through his hair, considering. "Maybe...maybe the race won't protect our pieces, but that doesn't mean we can't. We need to find our own protection spell."

Hope blossomed in me. That was a good idea. "Do you know a spell like that? That's powerful enough?"

"No, but I know someone who does. It's time we go see my father."

13

The walk back through the squares we'd already passed seemed so much longer now that I was carrying the weight of Peachkin's death on my shoulders. I barely noticed the streets turning from black to white and back again as we tramped through them, this time without our little companion.

I was hyper-aware of Ruth walking behind us with her camera. She'd filmed it all—Ario's sword slicing through Peachkin—the leprechaun's green blood leaking onto the cobblestones. Yes, we were being filmed. Ruth hadn't left our side for a second, but did they really intend to air that footage? This race had turned from a harmless reality TV show into something much more terrifying. The rules didn't apply anymore.

A chilling thought struck me. What if the studio wasn't in charge anymore? What if the Brotherhood and King Obanstone had taken over? I kept the sentiment to myself. It didn't change anything. We needed to play along if we had any hope of discovering the last anchor point and thwarting the Brotherhood's scheme.

As we walked past the library, it took everything I had not to go back inside and speak to my mom again. I longed to see that she was still all right, but we needed to go see Orin's father more. It was the only way we'd be able to protect her if the fight came to her. Still, as we passed the doors, my heart ached with a pain so raw that I had to take several deep breaths in an effort to swallow the feeling.

Orin gripped my hand more tightly, and I swore I heard him whisper that we'd get her out. It was so quiet, it could have been the wind, and with Ruth following so closely behind, I didn't want to ask him to repeat it. It comforted me, nonetheless.

We passed over to the black square and began our hunt for our king, Orin's father.

In the last square, the library had been the obvious choice as it was the biggest building in that area, but this square had nothing obvious. Peachkin had made himself known on the first square, but looking up and down the empty street, it was clear that Orin's father wasn't going to do the same.

"Which way?" Orin asked, glancing both ways at the T-junction that marked the border between squares.

I shrugged my shoulders. They both looked the same and as there were no defining features about either direction I figured it didn't really matter. "You choose."

We turned left and walked up the street. Here there were no shops, just rows of pretty little cottages. It was so sad that they were all now deserted, their owners having been ordered to leave. They were yet another victim in this supposed game.

"Where do you think all the people are?"

"What people?" Orin asked without breaking a stride.

"The people who lived here. There must be over a thousand displaced families because of this race."

"If you worry about that on top of everything else, you'll go mad. Let's just pretend they're all on ...vacation somewhere. It's easier that way, and we don't have to say any more on the subject."

He was right, of course. I had enough on my plate with trying to keep myself, my sister, and my mother alive and stop faerie Armageddon. I didn't need to take on more worry about perfect strangers. But I couldn't help it. How many people had the king hurt to get what he wanted? The guy was ruthless.

We, on the other hand, were not Ruth-less. She was behind us filming every word I said so I elected to do what Orin said and keep my mouth shut.

After walking through the streets for a while, we came upon a small village square. In the center was a statue commemorating some local hero, and on the steps below it, a newspaper in hand, sat a faerie male. It must be Orin's father.

When he saw Orin, he dropped the paper and strode over to us. "Orin, my son, you have done me proud."

He was a tall male with Orin's same dark features, albeit with bushier eyebrows and a thick black mustache. He looked a little like a faerie Tom Selleck. His jet-black hair was streaked with silver. He held out his hand for Orin to shake, but Orin grabbed it and pulled him into a hug. I grinned at the shock on his father's face as his son held him tightly. Something told me that this was the first hug that these two males had ever shared. At least one good thing had come out of this ridiculous race.

I thought I saw a tear glimmer in the male's eye, but as he pulled out of Orin's embrace, he coughed and pulled a handkerchief from his coat and dabbed it away. He turned to me, and this time, when he held his hand out, I shook it rather than hugging him. I had a feeling one hug was enough for him to cope with.

"Fine looking partner you have, Orin," he said. He turned back to me. "And a feisty one too. I've been watching you both on the show, and I have to say, I never thought a human would get as far as you have. I tip my hat to the pair of you. My name's Octavio, by the way. I thought I should introduce myself, seeing as Orin forgot his manners."

"Pleasure to meet you, sir." I didn't exactly love being called a "fine looking one" like I was a prize cow, but I supposed his other compliments made up for it. And things were different here in Faerwild, right? I chose to give Octavio the benefit of the doubt.

"What's that?" he shouted all of a sudden, gazing over my head, shock written across his features. "Did the other team follow you? I just saw them running down the street. A dragon was chasing them, but I think they lost their camera person."

I turned around in alarm. If Tristam and Sophia were here, the game was definitely rigged. And a dragon? Again? All I saw was Ruth who'd spun her camera around quickly to capture the action.

The street was empty, but a huge roar filled the air, making my heart hammer in my chest. Why had I left Ario's sword behind?

"What should we do?" I asked, turning to Orin in a panic. He was surprisingly calm about the situation.

"I think we should leave them to it. Although, watching the crown prince get burned to a crisp would make great TV," said Orin, speaking loudly.

I saw a sly look pass between father and son. What was going on?

"Shame they don't have their camera person to capture it," Octavio added.

That was all Ruth needed to pelt off after them. She ran across the square and around the corner so fast it was almost as if her shoes were on fire.

When I turned back to the males, they were laughing. "Is anyone going to tell me what's going on?" I demanded.

"There's no dragon, right?" Orin asked.

"I very much doubt it. The roar was just a little bit of tomfoolery on my part. Hopefully, it will keep her away long enough for me to speak to you. Here, come look at this interesting article I was just reading in the paper."

Thoroughly confused, I followed the two males back to the statue where Orin's dad picked up the paper he'd dropped. He retrieved it and held it out in front of him.

"Come closer," he whispered. We did as he asked and moved behind him so that we were looking over his shoulder and the three of our heads were practically touching.

"The paper is the only way to hide from the cameras," he whispered. "See what I mean. Robots, eh?" he shouted out a little too loudly. He lowered his voice once again. "We need them to think we're looking at an article, so play along."

I nodded my head. "Robots are a growing trend," I said clearly and loudly.

Octavio's handsome face grew serious. "You two need to get out of Elfame. Get out now, and by whatever means you can."

Orin recoiled slightly. "We can't. We're so close. Winning is the only chance I have to free you and Mother from your servitude."

Octavio shook his head so violently that the paper shook in his hands. "No, son. The game is rigged. It's always been rigged. You will not get out of it alive if you keep playing. Now, you can't go forward because a magical field will always block your path, but there is nothing stopping you from heading back off the edge of the playing field. Go far away. Go to the human realm if you have to."

"If we don't win the race, you and Mother will be the king's slaves for another eighty years. If he even lets you go then! He seems to rely on Mother's magic."

Octavio growled. "The fate of two faeries is inconsequential in all this. You mother and I have agreed that you are more important. They plan on bringing together our realms, and if they do that, the consequences will be dire. Just get out while you still can."

I chimed in. "We already know that. That's the other reason we can't leave. We know the Brotherhood has MEDs planted and there's one nearby, somewhere in the old city. We're looking for it." I opened my eyes wide. "Do you have any idea where it might be?"

Octavio shook his head. "Though Ramona did overhear something important. Those MEDs are more dangerous than you even realize," Octavio said. "To trigger the magic spell component of the explosive, there must be a sacrifice. Of human blood. Whose blood do you think they'll go after?" He turned and gave me a pointed look, but before I could answer a scream rang in my ears. Dropping the paper, we all looked up to see Ruth racing across the cobblestones, this time her camera hung at her side rather than sitting in its usual place on her shoulder.

She screamed again, but her voice was lost in a buzzing roar. My eyes flew open. There was what could only be described as—a *horde* of bees behind her. A swarm of bees would be scary enough, but this was clearly no ordinary swarm. The mass of them wove together and morphed to form a face like a laughing skull. I'd never seen anything so spine-chillingly horrific in my whole life.

"Time to go," Orin said, gripping my hand and pulling me and his father away from the monstrosity. No matter what Octavio had told us, our path out of here was cut off. It was further into the game or death by killer bees. It wasn't a hard choice. I sucked in a deep breath and ran away from certain death.

14

"In here," Octavio called, gesturing towards a two-story house bordering the square. It looked like Snow White's cottage, complete with a thatched roof. I realized as we threw open the door and piled inside that thatched roofs might not be impervious to bees, but it was too late.

"Come on!" Orin shouted at Ruth, who was running as fast as her little legs could carry her. Behind her, the horde of bees reared up, as if it was about to grab and swallow her whole. I hoped that whatever protective enchantments the race promised her would hold.

She made it through the door just seconds before the swarm. Orin slammed the door shut, and the bees slammed against it with the force of a thousand bullets. More threw themselves against the windows, covering the panes with their vicious little bodies crawling and scraping, blocking out the light.

"Do we think those will hold?" I asked nervously, backing up. More bees seemed to be arriving by the second.

Octavio swept his hands around the cottage, and a purple sheen appeared, coating the walls and ceiling. It must have been some sort of shield. "That should hold for a few minutes."

"What the 'ell is goin' on?" Ruth asked, her red hair wild and sticking up from her head. She had apparently forgotten that she was supposed to be observing and filming, as her camera was hanging limp in one hand.

"I think this means it's your turn," Octavio said, turning to us. "This is supposed to...motivate you to make your moves quickly."

"What happened to the gong?" I cried. Jesus, first poor Peachkin and now this? This race was going way off the rails.

Octavio shrugged helplessly. "Maybe the producers worried the gong was too boring."

"Boring?" I screeched, raising my voice to be heard over the incessant hum of the bees outside. "A faerie just died. They can't give us a few minutes' peace?"

"A faerie died?" Octavio asked.

Orin nodded. "One of our pawns. That's why we came here. Our pieces aren't shielded like they're supposed to be. I wanted to ask you if you knew a shield spell that could be transferred to another person."

"Orin, give me the gameboard," I held out my hands. At least, I could make use of my time while Orin was getting instructions on the spell.

I examined the little board, trying to take stock of the location of all the pieces, and to think strategy. But I could hardly hear myself think above the killer bee swarm. A cracking sound made us all freeze. It was one of the front windows—a hairline crack was running up it, like ice on a frozen pond.

Then it shattered, and the mass of bees surged forward against Octavio's shield, bulging towards us.

"That's not going to hold for long," Octavio said, effort written across his face.

"If the swarm is to get us to make a move, then once we move, it will go away, right?" I looked at Orin then his father. They both nodded, a motion so similar that it would have made me laugh if our circumstances weren't so dire.

"Okay, then let's go!" I said, surging to my feet and grabbing the board. I thought I'd come up with a rough plan. "We're moving our king!"

"Ye wanna go oot there?" Ruth gasped. "In that?"

"Can you hold the shield around us?" I asked Octavio. "While we make a dash for it?"

"I'll make it work."

"This dunna seem like the time to tell ye I'm allergic ta bee stings," Ruth said. She looked absolutely petrified.

I huffed, frustration overtaking me. I didn't want her here. I didn't want to talk to her, to get to know her, to worry about her. I wanted Ben. But it wasn't her fault what had happened to him.

"I'll keep the shield around all of us," Octavio said. "We stick together."

We crowded around the closed door, ready to bolt. "We move on three," Octavio said. "One...Two...Three!" He blew the door off its hinges and out we ran, into the swarm.

It was like running through a tornado—or what I imagined running through a tornado would be like. There was a dark swirling mass of wings and legs and bodies around us, so thick I couldn't see past them. The sound of their angry buzzing drowned out everything else—even the hammering of my heart in my eardrums. It felt like an eternity as we ran blindly through the streets, headed for another square—and safety.

At last, we found it. We crossed from a black to a white square, and the bees stopped at the purple magical border, just as it had once stopped us. They hammered angrily against the force field of magic. I swore I could hear frustration in the tone of their buzzing. They didn't like to be deprived of prey. But for now, we were safe.

We collapsed to the stones of the street, me on my hands and knees, gasping for air, Orin with his head in his hands. Ruth was quietly sobbing. Octavio stood behind us with his hands on his hips, his chest heaving.

I patted Ruth awkwardly on the shoulder. "You're okay."

"I guess we were right," Octavio said. "The bees have vanished. I guess they were conjured to get you moving along."

I let out a long sigh of relief. At least, the FFR wasn't trying to kill everyone off. Just us, it seemed.

Orin looked at me and let out a tired laugh. "If you still want to be a stunt woman, all you'll have to do is show them the footage from this damn race at your auditions."

I barked out a laugh and fell back against the stones for a moment, catching my breath. Did I still want to be a stuntwoman? It seemed an eternity ago—a world away—that I had worked in a Hollywood studio, fetching coffees for asshole bigwigs. In reality, it was less than a month ago. I couldn't believe I had changed so much in such a short time. But I guess an experience like this did that to a person. Changed them.

"Where do we go from here?" Orin asked.

Looking down at the board, I saw that Niall, our bishop, was in a square nearby. Now that Octavio had shared a shielding spell with Orin, maybe it was time to see if we could figure out where the final anchor was. It seemed as good a time as any. Plus, he was a renowned chess player. Maybe he could help us out a little. "Let's go see our bishop."

Orin nodded, eying me shrewdly. I knew he understood the deeper meaning.

We said farewell to Octavio and promised him we'd return. He and Orin embraced, and I saw the reluctance in Orin's eyes to leave his father. It made sense. I'd felt the same just hours ago, leaving my mom. But Octavio would be all right. He had magical defenses, and no one was coming for him. Yet.

We found Niall in what looked like an abandoned restaurant, filled with empty tables and chairs. He sat in a green-leather booth, reading a book. A glass of whiskey sat on the table beside him along with a couple of plates of chicken wings. I hoped the whiskey was his first. Although, on second thought, maybe getting him a little sloshed would loosen up his tongue. It had seemed to work that way last time.

We slid into the booth across from him.

"Hello Niall," I said coolly. "It's been a long time."

"My young chess prodigies." He closed his book, setting it on the table. I squinted at the title, but it was in a language I couldn't read. "Have a drink. Have some food."

I picked up a chicken wing and devoured it right down to the bone, before picking up another. Who knew when we'd get fed again?

"Let's see how you're doing," Niall said.

"What?" Orin asked.

Niall gestured to the worn table before him. "The gameboard. Let's have a look. I'm not supposed to help; but I'll admit, I'm curious."

I sat the board down between us with a sigh. "It's not pretty. They're totally screwing with us. They aren't shielding our players, and they sent a swarm of bees after us to make us take our next move, so we botched it. It's like they want us to lose."

"All the more impressive if you win." Niall touched his nose and pointed at me, his eyes twinkling. Damn it, even if he was an evil Brotherhood member hell bent on ending human civilization as we knew it...I liked the guy.

"We need your help," I began.

Holding his hands up in front of him, he replied. "I cannot say too much, but I can let you know that rules are meant to be broken, and those that are being broken have nothing to do with me." He licked his lips and side-eyed the camera. "I'd...focus your energy on Evaline." He tapped on the glass bubble over the board.

"Evaline?" I asked, peering closer. I hadn't really paid attention to who Tristam and Sophia's pieces were. Evaline, our former magic instructor, was their bishop... and *Gabe* was their king? "Why is Gabe their king?" I asked, looking at Niall accusingly. "Orin's father is our king. It should be..." Oh, of course. Tristam's father wasn't going to deign to involve himself in such a petty little game. He was more than happy to pull the strings like a puppet master, but he couldn't be troubled to actually get his hands dirty.

Orin's face darkened. "I feel like a broken record, but that's not fair."

Their queen looked to be a short, curvaceous black-haired woman that I assumed was Sophia's mother. At least they had one family member to worry about.

"You must know by now that the race isn't an entirely... level playing field."

"Understatement of the year," I said.

"I'd spend less time complaining and more time figuring out how to even the field. If they're going to cheat, you should cheat too."

I avoided looking at the camera, wondering if he was trying to goad us into doing something that would get us kicked out. I had no reason to trust him. No reason at all. "We'll take the high road," I said. "We don't need to cheat to win. Unlike other teams." Though in truth, what Niall said made sense. Orin and I did need to look for any chance to one-up our competition. I wasn't above cheating if it kept my mom alive and found us the anchor point.

"That's your choice, of course," Niall said. "Quite admirable, actually. You're definitely the fan favorites out there." He gestured into the air, which I assumed referred to the human world.

"Really?" Orin leaned forward.

"Yes, definitely. But don't let it go to your head. It's anybody's race. And don't assume you've seen the last of their tricks. I assure you, the Faerie king will want to end the race with a bang."

Orin and I exchanged a meaningful glance. A bang? Like...an explosion? If Niall said that, he must know what the king had planned.

"Do you have any idea what he's planning?" I asked, trying to feign nonchalance. "I'm sure he's feeding Tristam intel. It'd only, as you said, level the playing field."

"I'm sworn to secrecy." Niall shook his head. "Oh look, it appears your competitors have moved. Our turn. I can't move yet as you can plainly see, but I'm enjoying sitting here and drinking my whiskey so don't feel the need to rush back. Good luck with the game. Chess is a noble pursuit, indeed. Play well."

Orin and I slid out of the bench, standing.

As he walked before me out of the restaurant, I whispered in Orin's ear. "He knows something. We need to find a way to get him alone. No cameras."

Orin nodded. "Agreed."

15

I was a competent chess player. If Tristam and I were sitting across from each other with a set between us, I was confident that I could have kicked his ass. But with killer bees, my mother in danger, and whatever the FFR producers would throw at us next, our strategy needed to change. I had to give up on playing this like a normal game of chess.

Move after move, we walked and walked. The playing pieces were all over the place—any semblance of strategy had flown out the window hours ago. It didn't help that each time we wanted to move a piece, we had to trudge to their square, only traversing squares we'd already been through. It was a game of endurance more than chess, and by the time the sun began to dip in the sky, even I was exhausted.

"We need to eat," Orin complained.

We hadn't eaten anything for hours, and even then, it was only the chicken wings that Niall had given us. My own stomach was starting to grumble, and I had to concede he had a point. Still, I wanted to get to Evaline before darkness fell.

I had absolutely no reason to trust Niall. He was probably part of the Brotherhood, and I knew for a fact he'd been up to shady business with Patricia...but my gut feeling told me he knew something.

I looked around us. Shops lined the street we were currently on. "Look. Three doors down. There's a candy store."

"It was a candy store," Orin huffed. "Before the king cleaned this place out. My stomach feels like a black hole. I need more than candy." He was as tired and irritable as I was. Maybe more.

"Something's better than nothing," I said. Apart from Peachkin and the other pawn, no one had been taken all day. We'd been dancing around the other team, playing defensively rather than attacking. I wondered if Tristam felt guilty about Peachkin's murder. Unlikely. Maybe he just wasn't that good at chess, after all. I pulled on the door of the candy store and found it unlocked.

Inside the door, I found the store of my childhood dreams. Glass bottles bursting with candy filled shelves lining the wall from ceiling to floor. My stomach gurgled again, this time in anticipation.

Running to a nearby shelf, I grabbed a jar with some sort of chocolate inside. Unscrewing the top, the smell of mint and milk chocolate filled the air. I put my hand in to grab one of the tasty treats when something stopped me. The thought of the doll in the DM shop earlier on in the day popped into my head. These sweets might look harmless enough, but I'd been in the FFR long enough to know that nothing was as it seemed.

"This isn't like Honeydukes, is it?" I asked Orin.

"Honey candy is over there." He pointed to some bottles

near the back of the store. "Though I've been far too close to bees today to even think about honey. I think I'll stick to chocolate."

"Not honey, Honeydukes. You know, the candy store from *Harry Potter*?"

He looked at me blankly.

Seriously, what did these faeries read here? "Never mind. Is this candy magic somehow?"

"Oh. No, it should be fine."

Finally, a straight answer. "Fill up your bag then and let's get out of here."

We took what we could and headed back out into the street. I didn't need to look at the map again to know where we were headed next. We were going right to the very corner of the board where Molly would be waiting for us.

I wasn't particularly looking forward to seeing Molly again. It was fair to say we'd never really hit it off, but the way things currently stood, she was our best bet to get to Evaline.

We found her in a large cafe. She greeted us with her usual sour expression.

"It's about time you two showed up. Jacq, I thought you were supposed to be good at this game."

"Chess is a tactical game, not a game of speed," Orin said, echoing my words from earlier. I suppressed a smile and told Molly where we needed to go as Orin disappeared into the kitchen area of the cafe.

"That's halfway across the board!" she complained. "It'll take an hour, and it's already dark."

Almost as she said it, the sun slipped over the horizon. I'd been so desperate to get to Evaline that the time had sped by. "What do you suggest?"

Molly shrugged. "Play pauses overnight. I guess they don't want the four of you to be totally sleep deprived. I'm going to find somewhere to sleep. I'll meet you back here tomorrow." She left the cafe through the front door. I had half a mind to stop her, to tell her that we should stick together, but I held that thought. If her words were true, and the game did truly pause overnight, then we wouldn't need her until morning. And I didn't particularly want to stick with Molly if I didn't have to. Time to focus on getting a bit of food and rest.

The smell of bacon wafted over to me. Following it, I found Orin in the kitchen, cooking up a storm.

"Look what I found," he grinned, pointing to the pan that had bacon and eggs frying in there. Two thick slices of sourdough bread toasted in a nearby toaster. I breathed in deeply, inhaling the glorious smells. "I never thought of you as domestic," I said, slipping under his arm to give him a quick sideways squeeze. I finally realized the two of us were alone. Well, as alone as we were going to get, with Ruth here.

"I look excellent in an apron," Orin said, returning to his cooking after shooting me a wink.

I was leaning against the wall impatiently, thinking about how he would look excellent in just about anything—or nothing—when he slipped a plate of food into my hand. All thoughts fled from my mind.

I moved to the counter and wolfed down the food as fast as I could get it into my mouth.

"Eat as much as you like," Orin said, cracking two more eggs into the pan. "The fridge is fully stocked. We can eat here again tomorrow."

My bones still ached with weariness, but the meal picked me right up.

After Orin finished his own helping, we headed back into the street. It was now pitch black, the only light coming from the cafe itself. All the streets had streetlamps, but none of them were lit, and the fact that this was a black square only compounded the darkness.

A cold wind blew down the street, and somewhere a howl ripped through the night.

"Let's find a place to sleep," Orin suggested. The street we were on was mainly residential, so it wasn't difficult to find someplace with a bed. The door to the first house we came to was open, so we let ourselves in. Orin waved his hands and light appeared, illuminating a tiny living room and some steps. Ruth barged past us, taking the steps to the top floor two at a time.

"I'm gonna git some shut-eye an' I'm doin' it in a nice wee bed. Don' ye two think ye can git upta anythin', though. The cameras are always watchin'!" My mood blackened at the reminder.

Orin nodded his head towards the door, and without exchanging a word, we decided to leave her there. We walked back into the night, up the steps to the next house in the row. It was nearly identical to the first, but, at least here, we wouldn't have to share a bedroom with Ruth or sleep on the couch.

The bedroom was modest with a small double bed and a dresser. A pair of rumpled pajamas rested on the bed.

"I guess the king really got people out fast," I said, opening the dresser door. It was filled with clothes—one-half with smart dresses and the other with suits. "He didn't even give them time to pack."

"Ruth was probably right about cameras," warned Orin. I took his meaning, closing my mouth. I shouldn't be talking about the king. Not when he had control of the gameboard and could send a magical avalanche or typhoon at us at any second.

I hadn't heard the gong since before dark; it was still Tristam and Sophia's turn. "Molly must be right that the game halts overnight," I yawned, moving the pajamas and resting them neatly on the floor. I had nothing to sleep in, just one other FFR uniform and my jacket, and so I fell onto the bed fully clothed. Next to me, the bed sagged a little as Orin lay down beside me. I wanted to talk to him, to assess how our day had gone, to plot our plan for tomorrow, but as his arms wrapped around me, a heavy sleep overcame me.

What felt like moments later, the sound of a gong woke us up. Light filtered in through a pair of raggedy curtains, signaling that I'd slept much longer than it felt like.

"It's our turn," Orin said with a groan, dragging himself out of bed. "Let's get out of here before the FFR decides to speed things up."

I grabbed my bag and the chess board and followed him out into the street. A bellow reached my ears. It was Ruth, and next to her, was Molly.

"I bin all over this street lookin' for ye," she raged, pointing a stubby finger at Orin. "And this wee girl has bin worried sick aboot ye."

I looked over at Molly, who rolled her eyes, crossing her arms before her. Worried my ass. She was probably just upset we'd shown up at all, because it meant she had to do something.

"What about breakfast?" I asked weakly. My bag was still full of candy, but I needed something more substantial.

"Not on yer nelly," Ruth said, "Ye heard the gong. Time to be off. I ain't bein' chased by those hell bees again."

I hated to admit it, but she was right. Begrudgingly, our strange little troupe set off towards Evaline. Our trip would take us the full length of the gameboard, which would take us several hours. We had to keep moving to keep one step ahead of the FFR. If we stopped for too long, something was sure to pounce.

By the time we reached the correct square, my stomach had knotted itself into a small ball of hunger. The candy helped a little, but I'd eaten so much sugar I was beginning to feel sick.

As we passed through the field to our destination square, magical armor appeared on Molly's body, complete with a sword in her hand. I put a hand on her shoulder, pulling her aside from the others. I didn't like her, but I had to warn her.

"This armor is supposed to protect you, but it doesn't. Ario killed one of the pawns when his shield failed."

Molly rolled her eyes again in disbelief. "You're just trying to scare me. I was told that the shield would protect me, and I couldn't be hurt."

"Look at the sword you're holding," I pointed out. "Doesn't it look very real and very sharp to you?"

"It's magic. It's got to look real or what's the point?" she said. I could see she wasn't convinced.

I shrugged. "All right. I tried."

Evaline was waiting for us. She wore the black armor of the other team and was posed in a battle stance, her sword raised above her head. It was very un-Evaline like.

As we approached cautiously, she lowered her weapon. "How exciting is this?" she called, gesturing to her armor. "It just appeared. You coming into our territory must have triggered it. Did I scare you?" She gave a little laugh.

"Terrifying!" enthused Orin. I wanted to run over to her and hug her, but I restrained myself. It was strangely comforting to see her. Even if she was our opponent, it was nice to see another familiar face.

"I guess you took me, huh?" she grinned, seeing Molly with us. "Time for me to leave. My time is up."

That was it? She was just going to walk off the square? The stress I'd been carrying for the past twenty-four hours melted from my shoulders as I remembered that the people on both teams were real and not all were psychopathic killing machines. However much I hated Ario right now for what he did to Peachkin, he *had* seemed just as shocked at what happened as we were.

"Good luck you two. I have to admit I prefer watching this on TV than being in the thick of it." She waved and turned to walk away.

Relief flooded through me as she began to retreat. If this was how the rest of the game played out, I had nothing to worry about. I thought about all the other playing pieces. Most were people I knew, some were unknowns. Of the ones I knew on Tristam and Sophia's team, I couldn't peg any of them for murderers. Not even Ario if I was going to be honest. I doubt he'd want a repeat performance of yesterday.

Now that I knew we could take pieces without fighting, I looked down at the gameboard. I'd been playing defensively, not wanting to see any more bloodshed. Now that I knew everyone was safe, I could really begin to play. I was going to crush Tristam! Attack strategies were spinning through my mind when a blood-chilling yell made me look up. Molly was racing towards Evaline, her sword raised in attack. "What the...?" I said.

Evaline managed to turn a split second before Molly's sword speared her in the back. Evaline deflected the blow and struck out herself, shock etched across her features.

"Molly!" I screamed, running forward. "What are you doing?"

As the pair, locked in combat turned, I saw tears streaming down Molly's face. "I don't know. I can't stop it," she panted. "It's the armor." She slashed at Evaline and the point of her sword almost connected with Evaline's right arm. A purple shield bloomed to life around Evaline, protecting her.

"I'm so sorry," Molly wailed as she pulled back to strike again.

"I yield!" Evaline yelled as she jumped away from Molly's sword. Just when I thought the FFR couldn't fuck with us any more than they already had!

"Orin," I screamed as the two women slashed at each other, but he was one step ahead.

"Let's grab Molly," he shouted, running towards her. "And try not to get stabbed."

Easier said than done with the way she was flailing around, her sword swinging wildly. Dropping my bag and the chess set, I ran into the melee.

I had never in all my life been more grateful for all the training I'd forced myself through. I knew how to hold a gun and a knife, and more importantly, thanks to my MMA training, I could disarm someone quickly.

I dashed behind Molly, wrapping one arm around her torso, and grabbing the hilt of the sword with my other hand. It helped that Molly wanted to be disarmed. What didn't help was the magic binding her hand to the sword. As my hand closed around hers, currents of magic ran through me, electricity vibrating my body until my flesh was numb. And yet I held on, knowing that if I let go, the consequences could be deadly. Orin reached Molly's other side quickly, grabbing her other hand. She was like a thing possessed, twisting and writhing against our hold.

"I think we have to let Molly get a mortal blow on Evaline," Orin panted, his hands almost losing grip on Molly's arm.

"The hell you do," Evaline called, crouched in a defensive position.

He was right. It was like when Peachkin took the first of Tristam and Sophia's pawns. "Your shield is working," I called.

Orin and I looked at each other, and on a silent count, we let Molly go. Molly and her armor catapulted forward toward Evaline. I cringed as Molly's sword came down in a powerful arc, praying that Orin was right. Otherwise, we'd just killed Evaline.

Molly's blow rebounded off Evaline's purple shield, throwing her back to the ground. Molly landed on her ass, and with a whizzing sound, her armor disappeared, leaving her sobbing in a heap.

Orin and I ran forward to check on them, Orin falling to his knees by Evaline's side. "I'm so sorry," I said, trying to kneel down next to Molly, but she pulled away with a hiss.

The four of us sat on the ground in shock, unmoving but for our heaving chests. What the hell were we supposed to do now?

A distant sound made me look up. It was an FFR magical flying machine, headed our way. They were coming to take Evaline from the board.

"Come on," Orin grabbed my hand, pulling me to my feet. My knees almost buckled; I was still weak with shock.

"We can't leave them."

"Do you want to be here when the FFR staff land? This trial is getting stranger and stranger, and we just tried to foil their little spell. I don't particularly want to stick around to find out what they think."

A voice blasted out of a loudspeaker, emanating from the strange helicopter. "Jacqueline and Orin, stay where you are."

16

I looked sharply at Orin in alarm. Were we in trouble? Because we'd tried to stop Molly? Because we'd interfered? But Orin was right. Whatever they wanted with us, I sure as hell wasn't going to stay here to find out.

"Come on," Orin said, grabbing my hand. We turned on our heels and ran. I was gaining a sense of direction in this place, so I knew, generally, which way we were headed. Back towards the safety of our side of the board. Away from the madness of this square. We'd just moved Molly, so we had a little time while Tristam and Sophia made their next move.

I glanced over my shoulder and saw that Ruth was running after us. The FFR helicopter still followed. It had left Evaline behind and was coming for us. What the hell? What did it want?

We redoubled our pace, dashing through white-painted streets, through a quiet green park with a serene, tinkling fountain. "Maybe we should see what they want," Orin said, panting.

"No way," I replied. "This race has gone crazy."

"We can't hide from them forever," Orin argued.

"Worry about...forever...later," I said, pulling Orin sideways through an alley that was shielded from above by a large green awning.

"Down here," he said, and we headed down a set of stairs. "Please tell me this isn't the sewer..." I said, unable to stop myself from slowing down. The Elfame sewer seemed like the place blonde human girls went to die.

"No, it's the subway," Orin said.

"You have subways?" I asked, curious despite our predicament.

The staircase deposited us into a wide, white-tiled station. "This way," Orin said, and we darted through a tunnel onto a platform. There were no tracks in the tunnel, just what looked like pavement smoothed over into two grooves. "Where are the trains?" I asked.

"The cars are pulled by hellhounds. I'm assuming when they evacuated everyone for the race, they pulled the dogs out of here too."

"Hellhounds?" My fingers bit into Orin's bicep. "You assume they removed the dogs, or you know?"

"We either go forward, or we go back."

I looked over my shoulder, biting my lip. Demon dogs, or FFR staff? I huffed. "Okay. Go."

We jumped off the platform and jogged into the dark of the tunnel. It was eerily quiet, nothing but the pounding of our boots on the stone floor to keep us company. My breath was ragged in my throat, but not from the pace we were keeping. I felt sure that at any moment, a hellhound was going to pop out at us. That would be just my luck. I looked over my shoulder, sure I saw eyes shining in the dark. But perhaps it was just my imagination. I tripped over a crack in the stone, and it was only Orin's strong hands that kept me from faceplanting.

Seconds later, a purple flash exploded around us, burning my vision. I blinked to try to clear the after-image of the magic, slowing to a walk. "What was that? Are you okay?"

"Hey!" Ruth cried out in the dark. "The camera ain't werkin'!"

I had forgotten she was with us. But Orin apparently hadn't. "You better get it fixed," Orin said solemnly, though if I could see in the dark, I suspected I would see a barely-veiled smile on his handsome face. We tried not to tamper with the camera, but I could sense that the magic flash had been his doing. We needed to lay low, and we couldn't do that if Ruth's camera was broadcasting our location back to race headquarters.

"There," he pointed. "I see light. We're at the next station."

I wanted to weep in relief. In the oppressive darkness of the subway, facing the FFR producers was suddenly feeling like the smart bet.

When we emerged from the stairs into the daylight once again, I sucked in a huge breath of fresh air. But my relief wouldn't last long. We were exposed out here and needed to find shelter stat. "There!" Orin said. We circled around the side of a building in the direction he'd pointed. Orin held his hand over the knob of a rusted metal door, and something clicked. When he twisted the knob, the door opened.

I stepped inside and let my eyes adjust to the dim light filtering through shuttered windows. We were in a grocery store.

"Sweet," I said, heading for the fruit section to grab myself a banana. I grabbed the bunch and realized they were hot pink. I blinked a few times, thinking maybe the darkness and flash of magic had messed with my eyes, but the bananas stayed, well, pink. "Are these safe to eat?" I turned to Orin.

Orin nodded, and I offered him one. He took it and held it at his side. "Not sure how you can think about food right now."

I sniffed at it tentatively before taking a tiny bite. It tasted like strawberry banana. "It's the only thing I'm sure of right now," I managed, chewing. "That we need to eat."

"Okay, so what do we know?" Orin asked, turning to me.

"The producers are out for blood," I said helplessly. "They brought in our family to be pawns, they took out their shields, and now they're forcing the pieces to fight. It was okay this time because Evaline still had her shield. But if Tristam and Sophia take one of our squares..." The weird banana turned to ash in my mouth.

"What I don't get is why?" Orin asked. "This trial is getting out of hand with the killer bees..." he shook his head. "And why were the race staff chasing after us?"

"I don't know. Ratings?" I shrugged helplessly. It seemed a little extreme for network television. Fights to the death. This wasn't ancient Rome, after all.

"Faeries appreciate a certain degree of ruthlessness," Orin said. "I wouldn't be shocked to see something like this in Faerwild for entertainment. But it doesn't make sense from humans. The first trial made us face dangers from the environment. The second, well, I think the whole Merfolk business was an accidental clusterfuck. But now, it feels like it's the race producers themselves who are out to get us. Why?"

I raised an eyebrow, wishing, not for the first time, that I could speak telepathically. Maybe the Brotherhood was onto us, and they were trying to take us out. They'd been subtle before, disarming our rings. Perhaps now that they were so close to their goal, the time for subtlety was over. I wished I could talk to Cass. Maybe they knew something about what the Brotherhood was planning; whether they were behind this. Speaking of Cass...I did have a way to contact her...

I finished my last bite of banana and turned. "I'm going to find a bathroom." I walked to the back of the store, hoping to find someplace to be alone from Ruth. I discovered the bathroom in the corner and locked myself inside.

I pulled the mirror Cass had given me out of my pack. I flipped it open, tapping the glass. It started to hum quietly, vibrating with the telltale glow of magic.

It wasn't long before the glass began to fog, and an image took form. Cass. The sight of her soothed me, and my shoulders sagged in relief.

"Jacq? Are you okay?" she asked, concern etched across her features.

"Yes. No," I said, shaking my head. "I don't know. Things have gotten crazy in here."

"I know," she said. "This trial there's only a short delay, no more than half-an-hour. It's basically being broadcast live. I saw you make a run for it. The FFR producers are searching for you everywhere."

"Why?" I asked intently.

"They're telling the audience that some of the magic spells malfunctioned. That the race staff is trying to find you guys to get it sorted out, so things can continue."

"Do you believe that?" I asked.

"I believe that the spells are going haywire. I doubt it's an accident, though. I'd stay in hiding if I were you."

"We can't stay here forever. As soon as Tristam and Sophia move, we'll be flushed out. And Cass—"

"I saw," she said. "Mom's there. Auberon and Louis are working on a way to get her out, together with Octavio. Octavio's presence worries us, especially. It could be a sign by the king that he knows who our operatives are inside the palace."

"Does that mean they're in danger? Could Orin's mother be at risk?"

She rubbed her face with one hand. "At this point, I think we're all in danger. We haven't heard of anything strange going on in the palace. Right now, the weirdness is centered on the gameboard. It's like the race producers are ratcheting up the excitement to distract everyone."

"Distract..." I trailed off, realizing what she meant. "Do you think they're doing this all so we don't have time to discover the location of the final anchor?"

"It's not so far-fetched, is it?" she asked. "They can't take you out directly, it's too public. But as long as you guys are on the defensive, running around the board, protecting your pieces, the Brotherhood can complete the work they need to do undetected."

"We need to talk to Niall," I said. "We'll go tonight. Find a way to sneak away from Ruth. Speaking of...I should get back. Orin broke the camera, but I don't know how long it will take her to fix it. I should get back."

"Be careful, sis,"

"You too," I said. I went to close the compact, but I hesitated. "If you could get Mom out of harm's way, that would be huge."

"We'll do our best," she said.

I reluctantly closed the mirror, shoving it back in my pack. I used the bathroom, washed my hands, and splashed some water on my face. I needed to get my head back in the game. I needed to be stone cold. At this point, there should be nothing that could surprise me. Whatever they threw at us next, I'd be ready. I nodded at myself in the mirror. "You got this, Jacq. Game on." I gave myself a little shake and opened the door to the bathroom. And promptly let out a bloodcurdling scream.

17

———

Of all the things I'd seen and all the things I'd expected to see, my asshole boss, John, was not one of them. Yet here he stood, wearing his usual designer suit, holding what looked to be a TV camera in his hand.

"Calm down, Jacq. I came to see where my triple venti mocha chocka latte is."

My jaw fell open with the shock of his appearance. "You scared the crap out of me," I said, my hand pressed to my chest.

A grin crept across his face, making him look odd. John wasn't a grinner. Scowling came much more naturally to the man. "It's a joke, Jacq. Jesus, lighten up. I don't even know if a triple venti mocha chocka latte is a real thing."

"You take your coffee black with sweetener," I whispered, unable to focus on anything more important. John was so utterly out of place in this weird world that I wasn't quite able to wrap my head around seeing him in here.

If the creature from the black lagoon or the Loch Ness

Monster appeared outside the bathroom, I'd have accepted it—been prepared. John, not so much.

"Right, although I have gotten a taste for those doughnuts. Now that the money's rolling in, I can afford the best personal trainer." He patted his belly like it was a badge of honor.

I nodded weakly, wondering if the bathroom was actually a portal to *The Twilight Zone* and I'd somehow fallen in. "Why are you here?" I asked, looking over his shoulder. In the front of the store, I could see Ruth munching on bags of chips. Orin was nowhere to be seen, which put me on edge. I turned my attention back to John. "Scrap that. How did you find me?"

"I didn't. I found Ruth." He nodded his head in her direction. "She has a tracker fitted to her camera. All the camera crew do. It's how we know where you all are. It's been reported that her camera has malfunctioned, so I brought her a new one. It's easier than sending a repairman to fix it while you two are on the go."

There was no way in a million years that John would volunteer to come in here just to bring a camera. They were expensive pieces of equipment, but John wouldn't lower himself to do the job of a lackey. No, he left those jobs to people like me.

"Why are you really here?" My anxiety was increasing as I sensed I was being tricked somehow. Although for the life of me, I couldn't figure out what the angle was.

John's usual calm exterior fell away as he moved toward me. His eyes flicked upwards and to the side before settling back on me. "There are no cameras here, right?" He was worried about the cameras? Wasn't he in charge of setting them up? If anyone knew where the cameras were, it was him.

I shrugged my shoulders. How was I supposed to know?

"Listen," he began, pulling me even closer. "The king's magic is malfunctioning. The shields on your pawns, the way Molly's armor went haywire. He swears he's trying to fix the problems occurring on the gameboard, but that it's just taking a little time."

"And you don't believe that?" I questioned.

"No. I can't profess to be an expert on faerie magic, but I can smell a bullshitter a mile off."

I almost laughed at his description of the king. I probably would have if John hadn't continued talking.

"I think he's deliberately sabotaging you and Orin so that Tristam wins. Nepotism at its finest."

I nodded my head, suddenly understanding. The FFR producers never wanted any of this to happen. They wanted thrills and adventure, yes, but not bloodshed. Reality show murder was still a bit much for the human world. So, the show producers were at the mercy of the king...just as much as we were. I'm not sure if it was better or worse that John knew we were being screwed over. At least they hadn't guessed the real reason. Hopefully, Cass and the other ICCF members were still incognito.

"Is this why the FFR helicopters were telling us to stop?"

"Yes. We need to get you out of here. After the incident under the sea, there was serious talk of pulling the plug on the show. Only, the king convinced us to air the third trial—he swore that he would have control of things within his own city. But now things are going haywire again. It's too dangerous."

Since when did John give a flying fuck about my safety? "Why do you care? Surely this is making you a fortune?"

He shook his head. "We're already facing a slew of

lawsuits when this is over. The studio board has decided that letting you stay is too big a risk."

So it was all about money. They'd done the cost/benefit analysis, and the cost of continuing the show had grown too high. I opened my mouth to tell John exactly what I thought of his calculations, but Orin walked into view at the other end of the store, which calmed my nerves instantly. Was he discussing chip flavors with Ruth?

"Leaving is good for you too, Jacq. You come out now, even without finishing the race, you'll make millions in sponsorships. You're the most famous woman on the planet, and with your good friend John behind you, we'll go far."

Good friend John? I wondered if he'd forgotten about firing me a month ago or the way he treated me like shit when I served him coffee every morning.

"Stay in here," he continued, "and you're as good as dead. We have no control over the king, and it doesn't seem like he has much concern for human life."

"And if I die, you'll lose your cash cow, namely me."

He grabbed my arms, his calm demeanor now completely dropped. "The censors are crucifying us, Jacq. We're losing money hand over fist fighting them, but they won't let us air the show without some of their people coming into Faerwild and making sure everyone is safe."

I let out a laugh. This time I couldn't help it. "Like that's going to happen."

"My point exactly."

"So the show's not airing right now?" I asked. But Cass had just told me she'd seen it...

"Not on Earth. The studio won't release it to any of the foreign networks until the FCC approves it for U.S. viewership. I think it's still showing in Faerwild."

Ah, that explained it. I thought for a moment about how

complicated this was all getting. There was the king and the Brotherhood trying to merge the fae world with the human world, Cass and her friends trying to stop him, and then in the middle of all this, there was poor old John and his cronies still trying to coordinate this stupid race even though it wasn't even airing on TV anymore.

The whole house of cards was crashing down, and yet, all of us caught up here in Elfame still thought we were doing this for a reality show.

"If it's not airing anymore, why don't you just cancel? Call the whole thing off? Pull everyone out, including us?"

He shook his head wildly. "Don't you think I've tried? The king won't let us. We're not steering this ship anymore and as far as I can see the ship is headed for the rocks. No need for you to go down with it."

"I'm not leaving." I said, trying to keep my composure. My mother was trapped in here. Whether or not we were on TV had never mattered to me. There were innocent people trapped on this game board, my mother being one, and I wasn't leaving without her.

"Jacq, come on! Think of the money! You want to be a stuntwoman? Forget it, you're so famous, you could be the leading lady. You'll have the pick of the parts, they'll make the prize money look like chump change. I've got seventeen contracts on my desk back at the office, just waiting for you to sign them. Tom Cruise has been calling my office daily to get you on board his latest flick."

"I don't care. I'm not coming with you. I'm going to finish this race."

"Why?" he asked, his face wrinkling in confusion. Maybe he'd missed his most recent Botox session with all the show stress. "I told you it's rigged and not even airing right now. You'll be committing career suicide staying in here, and that's if you don't end up dead."

I held my ground. "My mother's in here, unprotected. And Orin's father. And…"— I ground my teeth—"Molly and Niall. We can't abandon our pieces. If we just walked off, what's to stop Tristam and Sophia from taking them? They'll be undefended. I'm staying until this thing finishes." So much of me yearned to take him up on his offer. To walk out of here and never look back. But there was too much at stake here in Elfame—too many people I loved here in Faerwild. My mother. Cass. And Orin. If I went with John, how would I get them back? Not to mention, we still needed to thwart the Brotherhood's nefarious plot, or there'd be no lucrative sponsorships, no piles of cash. There'd be nothing but servitude to a mad faerie king.

"It's your funeral," John said quietly, shaking his head. It was like he was imagining me tossing kerosene on a pile of money and lighting the match.

"I know what I'm doing," I said quietly. "Will the FFR staff leave us alone? Not interfere?"

He gave a curt nod.

"Good. Now if you'll pass me that camera, I'll make sure Ruth gets it." I picked up the camera and headed to Ruth and Orin at the front of the store, not looking back. Dropping the camera at Ruth's feet, I grabbed Orin's hand and pulled him out of the store. My heart was hammering in my chest.

"What's happening?" he asked as I pulled him back into the subway. Ruth was hot on our heels, but she wasn't close enough to hear me. I told Orin everything John had told me including about the tracker on Ruth.

"We need to ditch her," Orin said.

"That's what I was thinking. Poor woman. Following us

around carrying that camera, filming our every move with no one to watch it."

Orin shook his head. "Not no one. I'll bet the king's boon that he's watching it. He'll want to know where we are at all times. We'll never truly be away from him until we get rid of the camera."

"Sooner rather than later."

He tightened his grip on my hand and took off running. We ran down the stairs of the subway quickly, once again descending into the dark. This time, I didn't worry about hellhounds, only Ruth, who was shouting our names behind us.

"This way," I hissed. We took the tunnel we'd originally come down and retraced our steps. Ruth would think we'd headed the opposite direction. Once the darkness completely swallowed us, we came to a stop, letting the blackness cloak us. In the distance, I could hear Ruth shouting for us, but her voice was getting quieter, as though she was moving away from us. When we could barely hear her, we set off again, this time at a brisk walk rather than run.

Then I heard what could only be described as a growl. I turned my head to find a pair of red eyes. Red eyes that were looking right at me.

18

"Orin," I hissed. Another pair of red eyes blinked open in the darkness, the low growls vibrating through my chest. "Please tell me hellhounds are friendly doggies."

"They are vicious creatures that are impervious to magic. They can only be controlled by the whistle of their handler."

"Can you conjure a whistle?" I asked as we both backed up slowly.

"No," he whispered. "I've never seen one, so I won't be able to."

"Any other way to stop them?"

Two more sets of eyes joined their friends. Holy crap—there were four of them.

"Find something stabby?" Orin offered weakly. "Faerie steel can kill them." Suddenly, I wished I hadn't dropped Ario's sword.

The lead hound stepped forward. The dim overhead lighting cast garish shadows on the beast, but I was confident that even on a brightly lit street next to an ice cream stand, this doggie would be scary as hell. It was almost as tall as I was at the shoulder, with skin as dark as night. It had no fur, just skin stretched over skeleton and lean muscle. Its mouth hung open and its breath puffed out from between wicked canines like steam from a volcano.

"Does it breathe fire?" I asked.

"Let's not find out," Orin said, backing up more quickly. The lead hound's muscles bunched as if to leap. "Run!"

We spun and darted down the dark of the tunnel, Orin throwing up a purple shield behind us. The hellhound leaped right through it as if it were nothing but a hologram.

"Shit," Orin said. The suckers were fast.

"What about conjuring a physical obstacle," I cried. "Like a wall. That would stop it, right?"

I could hardly hear the hellhound now, it was growing quieter. Were we losing it? I risked a glance over my shoulder and saw that it was literally feet from us. What the hell?

A brick wall manifested directly behind us, and I heard a yelp and a crunch on the other side. Then a snarl as the hellhound threw itself against the wall. Damn, that thing was strong.

"That won't hold it for long," Orin said. "Come on!" We sprinted through the tunnel, and I could swear the creatures' growls were getting louder.

I looked over my shoulder in panic. "It sounds like they're right behind us!"

"Oh, yeah," Orin panted. "The hellhound's growl is softest when it's right behind you."

Well, that was creepy as fuck. But it meant they were still blocked at the wall. I would have let out a breath of relief if I had any to give.

I saw a figure ahead, and a growl of frustration escaped

me. So much for losing Ruth. We'd just gotten ourselves chased by a pack of evil hounds, and now here she was again. "Run!" I cried as we pounded past her.

"Why?" she asked, but then a crash sounded behind us that could only be Orin's wall collapsing. Seconds later, I heard her panting along behind us.

"We need to find our piece on this square," I huffed. There was light ahead, which meant a station and stairs to the surface. "They'll have a sword."

Orin said nothing, which I took as agreement. A howl sounded behind us, which sent a chill scurrying up my spine. They were on the hunt.

We took the stairs two by two, bursting into the afternoon light. I spun in a circle, trying to get my bearings, while not keeling over from my lungs bursting. "Where are we?"

"The library!" Orin pointed.

I followed his finger and froze. The library where my mother was waiting. "No!" I cried. "We can't lead them to her."

"We don't have time to argue! We need her sword!" Snarls sounded at the base of the stairs, and Orin pulled me forward. I craned my neck and saw one of the hellhounds burst out of the subway station, its nose to the air.

"What the bloody hell!" Ruth wailed, her short legs pumping even faster.

Then the rest of the pack appeared, the four of them, a nightmare I'd never be able to unsee.

The doors to the library were just across the square, but the hellhounds were fast, their long legs eating up the distance between us. "We're not going to make it," I panted.

Orin threw a spell over his shoulder, and a tree standing at the edge of the square cracked and crashed directly in their path, separating them from us. It didn't stop them for long, the hounds just scrambled over the trunk, but it was the delay we needed to dive inside the library and throw the thick wooden doors shut.

"You faeries just had to have hellhounds pull your subway cars, didn't you. They couldn't be...unicorns? Or... golden retrievers?" I screeched at Orin, though I knew this wasn't his fault.

My mom appeared at the balcony where I'd first seen her. "Honey? What's going on?"

Something crashed against the doors behind us, nearly rattling them off their hinges. Another hit came, and the wood cracked.

Down the hallway to my left, I heard glass shattering. One of them must have come in through the window!

"Grab your sword, Mom," I screamed, pounding up the stairs. "We're leaving! Is there a back door?"

My mom darted into a room and came back holding a long sword gingerly like it was a poisonous snake. I grabbed it from her, determination filling me as soon as my fingers wrapped around the leather grip. Now things were a little fairer.

I grabbed my mom with my free hand and pulled her forward. "Is there a back way out of here?"

She stuttered for a moment before focusing. "Down there," she said, "past the kitchen."

We ran down a hallway, ignoring the sound of splintering wood and claws scrambling on marble tile. The growls were getting quieter.

We burst out the back door, and Orin somehow managed to thrust the stones from the ground behind us up into the air in jagged peaks, blocking the door.

"Where to?" I panted to Orin.

"I don't know," he said. "We can't fight off four of them with one sword. Maybe another square with our pawns?" But the squares were large, and we were dead on our feet. We'd never be able to keep outrunning them.

My mind spun for a solution, and I tried to shove down the voice that told me I should have gone with John. No. We'd gotten through worse than this before. We'd figure it out.

"Isn't there a way to stop them?" My mom asked, her short blonde hair in a wild halo about her head. "Calm them down?"

My eyes widened. "Could we find one of those whistles?"

"I told you I can't conjure—"

"Not conjure. Find one. In the...locker room for the conductors or something. Or...a pet store?" It seemed like whistles to control hellish dark hounds of doom would be the type of thing you'd find at a faerie pet store.

"Maybe," Orin said, closing his eyes and whispering under his breath.

Down at the far end of the library, one of the hellhounds exploded through the window, screeching to a stop, honing in on us. Another hound leaped and followed it through with more grace, also setting its red eyes on us.

"Orin..." I grabbed his arm, backing away.

"A minute..." he said, scrunching his brow in concentration.

"We don't have a minute..." I let go of him and gripped the sword in both hands as the hounds crept closer.

"Got it!" he cried, his eyes flying open. "This way!"

So we ran. I pumped my legs faster than I ever thought possible, pulling my mom, bodily, beside me. The hounds bayed behind us in the delight of the chase.

Orin threw object after object at them, slowing them slightly. His magic must be near depleted by now.

"There it is!" Orin cried as we approached a tidy brick building with a hanging sign. I didn't care what the sign said; I just knew it was shelter. My legs and lungs were burning, and I could feel my mom flagging beside me. We couldn't keep this up.

We piled inside the building, and Orin slammed the door shut. I looked through the windows to see the hounds screech around the corner and come to a stop, sniffing the air. One looked right at me, and I swore we made eye contact. I ducked down. Thank god, the windows of this store were barred. But the door was just wood. It wouldn't hold for long.

"What is this?" I turned to look, taking it in. It *was* a pet store.

"We're looking for a whistle," coughed Orin, his hands on his knees. "It stops the hounds. Fan out."

Orin, Ruth, and Mom moved through the aisles as I dragged myself before the door, sword in hand. It shuddered as a massive weight crashed against it. I licked my lips, trying to summon my courage. Just like the jaguar. Or the dragon. Or the merfolk. I'd faced faerie monsters before, and I'd bested every one of them. I could do this—

The door exploded inwards, knocking me off my feet. The sword clattered from my hand, and I scrambled for it in the debris. A hellhound filled the doorway, growling its near silent growl. I could feel the heat from its gaping mouth.

It took a step towards me, and my hands closed around the sword hilt. I pulled it up and with one fluid motion stabbed the hellhound through the neck.

The hound thrashed and reared back, wrenching the sword from my hand. It stumbled out of the shop, crying and screaming, dark blood pouring from its neck. Another hound appeared in the doorway, its baleful red eyes affixed on me. It bared its teeth at me—it knew I had just hurt its friend.

I scrambled away, my back hitting a shelf behind me. "Orin!" I screamed. I didn't have the sword anymore. I didn't have anything. I tried to fumble inside myself for my magic, but I was too terrified. The hound stepped closer, and its muscles bunched to pounce. I squeezed my eyes closed, bracing myself for the pain.

A piercing whistle cut through the haze of my fear. I peeked one eye opened and saw the hellhound standing still, its ears perked forward at attention.

Orin stepped forward, a silver whistle to his lips, the chain of it around his neck and a cardboard package in his other hand. He was reading the instructions!

He blew the whistle again, letting out two short bursts. The hellhound sat obediently. I let out a shaky laugh, burying my face in my hands as the adrenaline drained from me, leaving me hollow and exhausted. He'd done it. We were safe.

Orin blew three sharp whistles and one long one, and the hound rose, turned on its heel, and trotted out of the store.

He knelt down by me, his hands roving across my face, hovering over my body, checking me for injuries. "Are you all right? Are you hurt?"

I sprung at him, pulling him into my arms. I sobbed into his neck, breathing in his scent of herbs and pine and Orin. Finally, I pulled back, wiping my eyes. "I'm okay. You did it."

"We did it," he said, his dark eyes gentle as he offered me a hand and pulled me up. "If you hadn't stabbed that one we'd never have had time to find the whistle. Ruth found it, actually."

"Nice job, Ruth," I said, nodding to her.

"Anytime," she ran a hand through her red hair, shaking her head.

"Mom, you okay?" I asked.

"I think so," she said, pressing a hand to her chest. "That was quite an adventure."

"You don't know the half of it."

"Let's get out of here," Orin said.

We stumbled over the shards of the door into the beginnings of twilight. This day had felt like a hundred. I didn't think I could do anything more than collapse in a bed.

The one hellhound I had stabbed had fallen still beside the building. It was dead. Motionless and quiet, it didn't look so ferocious. I was sorry it'd had to die. But it had been it or me. And I'd always choose me.

I pulled the sword out of its neck gently, letting the black blood drip down the slick blade. I'd find something to clean it with before returning it to my mom.

"What's that?" Mom said, squinting into the setting sun. I lifted my head wearily.

There was something in the sky. No, not something...Someone.

Tristam and Sophia. Riding a white Pegasus. It took my haggard mind a moment to make the connection. Why were they here?

Orin was faster, he was already pulling the game board out of his pack, looking at it frantically.

Dulcina's shining hooves landed on the square across from us, and Tristam and Sophia hopped off.

"What's going on?" Mom asked.

Horror welled in me, stronger than I'd felt even with

four hounds of hell facing me. "We...moved," I said weakly. In our mad run from the hounds, we'd crossed a square. It had been our turn, and we moved. We'd exposed our queen.

The Pegasus shimmered and transformed into Dulcina's slim form. A sword flashed in her hand. The look on her lovely face was sorrowful. I think that was the worst part of all.

My mouth went dry as I grabbed my mom's hand, squeezing tightly. "She's here to fight you."

19

—————

lmost as soon as I'd uttered the words, brilliant lavender armor covered Dulcina's body, materializing as if from nowhere.

"Stay back," I warned, even though I knew my words were useless. Dulcina couldn't stay away even if she wanted to and judging by the pained look on her face, she very much wanted to. "I don't want to kill your mom, Jacq," she said, taking a step forward, "But I have to take this square. I don't have a choice."

Beside me, I saw my mom readying herself out of the corner of my eye. She didn't know the fight was going to be a real one. She still thought this was all just a game...a bit of fun for the cameras. We'd been so busy running away from hellhounds that I hadn't had time to warn her, and now it was too late. Dulcina lofted her sword in the air and charged for my mother.

"It's real," I screamed as Dulcina began to pick up speed. "What?"

She was closer still, heading for Mom at a dizzying

speed. She wasn't just fast as a Pegasus; she was speedy as a human too.

"I said..."

Closer.

"This is all..."

Almost upon us.

"Real." I pushed my mother out of the way, sending both of us spinning to the ground, the clatter of metal upon stone echoing in my ears.

Dulcina barreled past, missing her mark.

"Jacq," my mom admonished once she'd recovered from her surprise. "I'm supposed to fight. I know what to do. If I hit her shield, I can stay in, but if she hits mine, I have to leave. Not strictly legal in a real game of chess. Your father would be rolling his eyes if he was in here, but this whole race is a little far-fetched."

As my mom rattled on, Dulcina had come to a stop and was now turning, ready to attack again. I pulled my mom to her feet. "Sweetie, it's all right," she said. "The swords aren't even real. They're like some kind of magic hologram. They can't hurt me."

Dulcina ran towards us again, the blade in her hand looking as real as my mother's blade.

I grabbed Mom's wrist to pull her away. As far as I could see, running was our only option, but my mother wouldn't budge.

"The swords are real, Mom!" I screamed, willing her to move. "You saw what I did to the dog with it. That blood is real blood."

She shifted her position, and for a second I thought she'd seen sense and was going to come with me, but the clash of metal on metal over my left shoulder told me it was too late. She was already embroiled in the fight, and I was right in the middle of it.

"Jacq, I'm so sorry," Dulcina said, her face glistening with sweat. It looked like she was trying to fight against the armor—but with little success. Dulcina mumbled to herself as she lifted her sword to strike again.

This time, my mother was the one to push me out of the way. Her face had gone white. I think that first clash of swords had finally shaken some sense into her. "I'm protected, but I don't know if you are," she panted as she parried Dulcina's strike.

I ran forward again, intent on splitting them up, but a heavy hand grabbed my upper arm and pulled me back. "You'll get killed if you barge into the middle of them with no plan. You don't even have a weapon to defend yourself." Orin was right, but it wasn't his mom out there fighting. I was willing to bet if it was Ramona out there sparring with what for all intents and purposes was a lethal magical killing machine, he'd change his tune.

"Do something!" I hissed. My mother was holding up a lot better than I'd expected. Dulcina had received combat training during our month at Hennington House. We all had. My mother, on the other hand, was trained in selling insurance. Hardly something that would come in handy in this situation.

Orin didn't reply, and for a second, I thought he hadn't heard me, but when I turned to look at him, his eyes were closed, and his lips were moving in some kind of incantation.

There was a flash of purple light, and both swords turned into rubber, leaving them both wobbling in a comical fashion. The fight was now no longer lethal.

I laughed out loud in relief as the pair of them hit each

other with the rubber swords, inflicting no damage. My mother's laugh filled the air as she really went to town on Dulcina, showering down hits on her shoulders and arms. Even Dulcina's face had cleared of the worry, and a small smile had appeared on her lips as she realized that the fight had turned into something to have fun with.

"Thank you," I whispered.

Orin's hands interlaced in mine, sending jolts of desire through me. My adrenaline had turned into something else entirely, now that I knew my mother was safe.

"I know you were worried about your mom, but I think Dulcina's taken on more than she bargained for."

She was now cowering with her hands over her head, and my mother rained down blow after blow on her. Only the laughter coming from somewhere under her arms told me that she was enjoying the game as much as my mother was.

"I think I won!" My mother turned to us and raised her hands in a triumphant manner.

Dulcina stood and bowed down to her before holding her hand out for a handshake.

I blew a breath out. The fight had come to an end almost as quickly as it had started. But then I frowned. According to the board, Dulcina was technically supposed to win this bout. Was it possible for my mom to be the victor? Would she stay on the board? But two chess pieces couldn't occupy a single square at once without one taking the other...so would Dulcina leave? I wondered what we had to do next.

"We should return to the last square," I said to Orin. This new turn of events didn't sit well with me as it skewed the rules of the game. I was pondering all of this when Dulcina reared back with a gasp. A ragged scream ripped from her throat, and a ball of magenta energy began to form around her right hand.

"Shit!" Orin said, gripping my hand even more tightly.

Terror formed within me, and though I didn't fully understand what was going on, I knew by Orin's reaction that it was bad. My first thought was that Dulcina was sick or injured, but as the ball of pink energy began to intensify, I figured it out. That sphere of light was magic, and Dulcina was going to hurl it at my mom.

As with any magic, I had no idea what it would do until it reached its target, but the look of panic on Dulcina's face was enough to tell me that it wasn't going to be good.

"Help me," she screamed as the ball of energy flew towards my mother, hitting her right in the chest.

My mom let out a heart-rending scream as the magic hit her, knocking her off her feet.

"Mom!" I cried, running over to her, kneeling beside her writhing form. "Orin, what was that? Is she gonna be all right?"

Orin was just steps behind me. "I don't know. Only Dulcina knows."

"What was it?" I screamed at her as I cradled my mother's head in my arms. Tears streamed down Dulcina's face, and she shook her head wildly. "I couldn't help it. I can't control it." The pink energy began to form again, and she gazed down at her hand as though it was somehow not connected to her.

I had to remind myself that she was only the puppet in all this. The king held the strings. Still, my anger was roaring within me.

"Dulcina," I shouted at her, trying to get her to focus. "What was the spell?"

"It's a pain spell," she shouted back. She stumbled back

and waved her hand about as if to outrun her own magic. "It will hurt but not damage. It's the illusion of pain."

I breathed out a sigh of relief. It wasn't ideal, but at least when this nightmare was over, my mother would walk away from it. "You hurting, Mom?" I asked softly.

"Like a bitch! Illusion my ass!"

I'd never heard my mother swear in my life. I wasn't even aware she knew any swear words until now, but I guess enough pain could do that to a person.

She tried to stand. I moved to help her, but she pushed me roughly aside. Her pain was evident as she unsteadily got to her feet, her teeth gritted together.

"What are you doing?" We needed to get out of here and quickly, but it appeared my mother had other ideas. She reached down and picked up the rubber sword she'd dropped earlier.

"I can't help it any more than she can, Jacq." Her words chilled me to the very core. She was being magically manipulated too. This was a fight to the death, had always been a fight to the death, and now my mother was going into battle with a woman who could cause pain with a flick of her wrist, armed only with a sword made out of rubber.

"Jacq," Dulcina called out again. This time there was an insistence to her voice, which was tinged with terror. "There's another one brewing, and this isn't a pain spell. I'm sorry. I think...it's deadly. I can't help it!"

I could only watch as my mother walked stiffly towards Dulcina, the useless sword sagging in front of her. The ball of pink energy around Dulcina's hand had darkened and now spit ominous sparks. Then she pulled back her hand and threw the energy straight toward my mother.

I watched as if it played out in slow motion. The abject

terror in Dulcina's eyes, the way my mother didn't even duck to avoid the inevitable ball of death hurtling towards her.

I screamed, unable to move. My own fear had me frozen in place, and yet, even if I moved, I was too far away to do anything. My only option was to stand by helplessly and watch my mother die.

A split second before the angry energy hit my mother, there was a flash of blackness, and the ball disappeared. It took me a few seconds to understand what had happened, and when I did, the relief I felt at my mother being saved turned into dread as I saw Orin's body crash to the ground. He'd jumped right in front of her, shielding her from the attack. And in the process, he'd taken Dulcina's spell right to his chest.

"Orin," I cried out weakly, disbelieving the scene before me. He couldn't be dead.

The spell on my mother and Dulcina was broken. Their armor had disappeared. The act of Dulcina hurling that spell must have marked her as the victor—the winner of this square. Even though it hadn't taken out its intended target.

My mother bent to check on Orin and Dulcina raced forward, her pupils wide and tears streaming down her face. I beat both of them to him, even though I'd started off the furthest away.

"It was a kill spell," Dulcina whispered. "I didn't mean to..."

My entire world imploded with the realization of what Dulcina was saying. Orin couldn't be gone. I couldn't lose my partner. My friend. My...love. Not now.

I couldn't speak, couldn't answer Dulcina. It wasn't her fault, but I couldn't articulate the words to tell her that. In that moment, all I could think about was Orin and the crushing weight that had descended on me.

My own tears fell freely as I turned Orin's body...no, Orin. He was more than just a body, he was everything. I turned him from the face-down position where he'd fallen.

He looked up at me in surprise, letting out a groan. "Wow, I'm really glad we got those whistles."

I hissed in a breath, my heart hammering, my body shaking uncontrollably.

"I killed you," Dulcina breathed.

Orin sat up gingerly, one hand to his head. "I think you killed the dog whistle." He held up a piece of blackened metal still hanging from his neck. "It must have deflected the spell."

Emotion overtook me. Something precious had been lost and now by some miracle had been given back. I grabbed his face in my hands and kissed him full on the mouth, pushing him back to the ground. Passion, mingled with relief, mingled with who-the-hell-knew filled me, taking my breath away as I rained kisses upon him, clinging to him as if he might be taken away from me again, and I was dreaming the whole thing.

He kissed me back fervently, matching my own insistence, the two of us melded together in our own dizzying world away from the Faerie king and the FFR and the rest of the world.

"Get a room, why don't you?" a familiar male voice spat out. I reluctantly pulled away from Orin and looked up.

Tristam and Sophia were standing there, and it seemed they'd been watching us the whole time.

20

———

I couldn't find the energy to care. Let Tristam and Sophia know about Orin and me. Let the world know. I would proclaim it from the rooftops. I had fallen head over heels for Orin Treebaum, and there was no denying it.

I extricated myself from Orin and pushed to my feet, straightening my jacket. "This needs to end," I said to Tristam, my voice low. "It's getting out of hand." I wanted to rail at the arrogant prince, to scream and shout, but I needed to try another tactic. Perhaps, he could see reason. Perhaps, he could influence his father.

I approached Tristam and Sophia slowly, with my hands out, like I was approaching a pair of wild animals. "The rules of the race have changed. Dulcina was forced to send a deadly spell at my mother. Orin almost died intercepting it. Don't you think this is getting a little...extreme?"

Sophia looked at Tristam uneasily, and Tristam himself rubbed his jaw, his eyes on the ground. So, they did think it was getting crazy!

"Let's end this," I said. "If the four of us refuse to participate, no one else will get hurt. Let's just be done. Declare a tie." We hadn't found the final anchor yet, but maybe if the race didn't finish, the king couldn't execute his final coup de grâce. Besides, after the hellhounds and Dulcina's spell, I wasn't sure we'd survive to find the anchor if we stayed in it.

Sophia narrowed her eyes. "Do you think we're idiots? That we'd agree to forfeit and then you two can swing in and finish the race?"

"We wouldn't do that. We just don't want anyone else to die," Orin said.

"The producers won't let us quit," Tristam said. "My father said they're the ones who are changing the rules, tampering with the spells. For ratings. They won't let us just walk off."

My mouth dropped open, and it took me a moment to close it. "Tristam, that's not true." I looked sideways at Ruth's camera, then at Tristam and Sophia's camerawoman. I leaned in to Orin. "Can you disrupt the cameras magically for a moment, so we can talk to them privately?"

Orin scrunched his mouth in a thoughtful expression that just happened to be freaking adorable. "I think so."

The sound of an FFR flying machine reached my ears, and I saw one in the distance. Come to get my mom, no doubt. We didn't have much time. "Do it," I said.

Orin closed his eyes briefly while I stepped closer.

"What's he doing?" Tristam stepped back, alarmed.

"He's disrupting the cameras so we can talk," I said, closing the distance again. I hadn't been this close to Tristam and Sophia since we'd been locked in the underwater cave in the Elemental Trial. But right now, neither of them looked particularly devious. They looked...scared.

Orin stepped in too. "One minute."

"The race producers aren't in control anymore," I said, my voice low.

"Hey!" Ruth called. "Tha camera's not werkin'."

"Mine either," the other camerawoman said.

I ignored them, continuing. "Your father is doing this, Tristam. He's lying to you."

"That's not true," he countered. "Why would my father care about tampering with the race? It's supposed to improve human/faerie relations. It doesn't do that if a bunch of humans die."

"The race was never about improving human faerie relations," Orin said. "It's a cover. Your dad's part of something called the Brotherhood. It's a group of magicians who want to destroy the Hedge. Merge Faerwild and Earth."

"That's mad," Tristam scoffed.

"Is it?" I said insistently. "Just think about it. Your father would be king over Faerwild and Earth. The humans would be helpless. Just tell me you've never seen or heard anything that made you suspicious...anything your father wouldn't include you on?"

Tristam's face was stony as he thought. I prayed I was right and that the king hadn't been as good at covering his tracks as he could have been. Auberon had discovered the king's plans. Surely, Tristam had seen something suspicious.

Tristam shook his head. "Why would he go to the trouble of something as public as the race if he wanted to do something nefarious? That doesn't make any sense."

"He needed access between Earth and Faerwild, to bring in supplies. Explosives. This was his distraction. There are five magical explosives hidden in Faerwild. The final one is somewhere in Elfame," I said urgently. "Please, Tristam, Sophia, I know we don't like each other, but this is bigger than our rivalry or the race. This is all of our futures." I looked at Sophia, trying to communicate with my eyes how shitty this would be for humans if this went down. No more Instagram or hair straighteners or Lululemon. She'd probably die on the spot without any of those things.

"We've been trying to find the MED, the explosive," I said. "But this damn board has had us running all over, and we haven't been able to find it." I'd been thinking a lot about it, and I finally articulated something that had been gelling in my mind. "I think the end of the race is the location of the final explosive. The other explosives were located at checkpoints from the other legs."

"This is insane," Tristam said. "You guys are nuts. You're just trying to mess with us, throw us off our game because we're winning."

The FFR copter was landing now on the far side of the square. We were running out of time.

Orin shook his head. "It's the truth. And a final sacrifice will be required, a human sacrifice." Orin and I suddenly looked at each other, as another thought took form. The king's haywire magic had been rigging the board in favor of Tristam and Sophia. If the final anchor point was at the finish of the race—and Tristam and Sophia won...it was just who the king needed. His son, who would never question his mad plan...and a human. Delivered right to his doorstep —faster than Amazon Prime.

"Ohmygod," I said, my eyes widening in horror. "Sophia, you're the sacrifice. The king wants you two to win this, to make it to the end."

"I'm not listening to your craziness," Sophia said, starting to back away.

A short, squat faerie with orange spiky hair was striding from the helicopter. "Mrs. Cunningham, we're here to take you back to Earth."

Tristam and Sophia were backing away from us. Our clandestine chat had done nothing but convince them we were fucking with them. How to convince them?

"Tristam," I said. "Your brother is alive."

Tristam's blue eyes widened in shock, his tan features going pale. "You're lying."

"I'm not. And I can prove it."

"Mrs. Cunningham," the faerie repeated, beckoning my mother with an outstretched hand. "Now, please."

I turned my attention to my mom, not willing to let her go without saying goodbye. I hugged her tightly. "You were so awesome, Mom. You totally kicked ass."

"You saved my life from those dogs," my mom said. "I'm proud of you. Be safe."

I pulled back reluctantly, looking at her sweaty and dirt-streaked face. "I have some good news for you when I get home, okay?" I pulled her into one more hug. "I found her," I whispered in her ear.

The faerie pulled my mom from me, towards the waiting helicopter. I could see the retreating forms of Tristam and Sophia running from the square with Dulcina out of the corner of my eye. But my gaze was fixed on my mother. Her eyes and mouth were open wide as she stumbled along, too weak with shock to resist. I smiled at her. "Say hi to Dad! Tell him I love him." I waved, forcing a smile, praying it wasn't the last time I'd ever see her. Because this race wasn't over yet.

21

────────

When the helicopter disappeared from view, we were very much alone. The three of us stood in silence, each of us reflecting on the last hour of our lives. Ruth's camera was now working again, but she made no move to pick it up and point it in our direction. I almost felt sorry for her. She hadn't signed up for this any more than we had. She'd signed up for a stable week or two's worth of work and a nice fat paycheck at the end of it. Instead, she'd run for her life, faced hellhounds who wanted to eat us, and a magical fight to the death.

To top it all, her presence here was basically pointless as the footage wasn't even being broadcast on Earth. I had half a mind to tell her to put her out of her misery. At least then, she could leave and still get the paycheck.

I set off slowly towards the edge of the square. Ruth grumbled something about it being bedtime and her legs being too knackered for this, but I ignored her. I had a plan, and Ruth's knackered knees didn't figure into it.

She was nothing but a burden to Orin and me. She ran much slower than we did so that we constantly had to slow down for her to keep up with us. It made hiking across the board tedious. Well, it would have been tedious if it wasn't for the constant fear of crazy monsters jumping out at us. Plus, with the chance that her recording could get back to the king, we weren't free to strategize or plan what came next.

"Where are we going?" Orin asked quietly as we walked across yet another square. Now that we'd been playing a while and our pieces were all over the board, it had opened up to us much more. As long there was one of our playing pieces ahead of us, we were able to keep moving freely through the squares to get to them.

"I want to go and see Niall," I whispered back so Ruth couldn't hear me. "I just don't want Ruth to know that, so I'm deliberately walking in the opposite direction."

"What are ye two whisperin' aboot?" huffed Ruth behind us.

"You know, I think I'm tired," Orin said, stretching his arms out. "Let's find a place to sleep."

We'd walked into a commercial zone, so there were no more beds like there had been the night before, but Ruth didn't seem to care as we opened a shop door and paraded in. The shop sold furniture, and although it didn't have any beds, it had a couple of comfy looking sofas. Ruth barged past us and collapsed on the biggest. She certainly took her comfort seriously.

"I guess we're sleeping here," I said to Orin, taking the much smaller sofa. I nodded over to Ruth. She'd already gotten herself comfortable and closed her eyes.

Orin waved his hand and threw a ball of light at her head. Moments later, she was snoring softly. "Sleeping spell," Orin said. "It should keep her down for a few hours."

A few hours' sleep. Oh, how I envied her. My body felt

like a lead weight pulling at me, my muscles shaky with exhaustion from our flight from the hellhounds. But we had bigger fish to fry, and I didn't see myself having the luxury of sleep in the near future. We left the store, pushing back into the faerie night.

Without Ruth holding us back, loping across the board was freeing. With the breeze in my hair and Orin next to me, I could almost believe we were on a date, instead of headed to see an alcoholic Brotherhood member, who may be our only hope of saving the world.

Orin grabbed my hand and pulled me into the shadows.

"What?" I asked, but he held a finger to his lips and nodded to the end of the street.

I followed his gaze. It was dark, and it took a while to see what it was that he was pointing at, but then I spotted it. A guard dressed in the palace uniform crossed the street. I held my breath as he walked in front of us, but he didn't see us. I waited until he was completely out of sight before speaking.

"I thought this was a bit too easy," I said, making a move to head back out into the street. Orin tugged me back, but instead of pulling me away from someone like he did last time, he pulled me towards someone. Him.

He was forceful as he pushed me back against the shop wall, falling right back into the kiss that Tristam and Sophia rudely interrupted. His hands were all over me, igniting senses that I didn't even know I had.

I pressed into him, matching his urgency, my heart pumping wildly, on the verge of exploding with the thrill of it all. I'd been kissed before, but this was something else entirely. I ran my hands down his back, and then to his ass. His perfect ass that right at that moment, I wanted to take a bite out of. I wanted all of him, to drink him all in, to lick and nibble, and feel his skin against mine. If we weren't in the middle of hell, I'd have ripped his clothes off right then and there, but we were and making out in the shadows, no matter how wonderful, was not going to get us out of here.

Orin reluctantly pulled away, his lips swollen, his breath panting. "We should get goi—" but he couldn't complete his sentence because I'd snaked my hand around the back of his neck and pulled him back into the kiss. Yes, I wanted to save the world, but fuck, it could wait a few minutes!

It was the sound of footsteps that finally broke us apart. The guard who'd walked down the street was now walking up it. Once again, he passed by without seeing us, but it meant we needed to find a different route. I couldn't help giggling as we stole down the alley away from the guard and headed onto the next street. There was something delicious about holding Orin's hand and sneaking through the city in the dark after the most passionate kiss of my entire life. If we both managed to get out of this alive, I was going to enjoy kissing Orin a whole lot more.

The exuberance I felt as we crept through the streets never waned, the joy of it carrying me the whole distance to Niall's square. It was only when we found the bar empty that reality set in.

"Where is he?" I asked pointlessly. If I didn't know, then neither would Orin.

"He can't have gotten far. There's still some whiskey left." He pointed behind the bar where rows of bottles stood, some unopened, some partially empty.

"It's late. He's probably found some nice place to sleep. The FFR must have made allowances for the playing pieces. They can't expect them to sleep on the floor or have to find a place like we have had to."

Orin nodded thoughtfully. "You're right. They would all

have been briefed on where to sleep, but all the pieces move, so they'd have to know the arranged sleeping spaces on each square. How many squares does a chess board have?"

I counted up manually in my head. "Eight across, so sixty-four."

"Could you remember the location of sixty-four places to sleep?"

"Right at this moment, I can barely remember my own name," I yawned.

"Exactly. There must be a marker or something. Something that sets the designated buildings aside from all the others."

"A marker visible in the dark?"

Orin nodded. "Yeah."

I'd been joking, but I supposed it made sense. The people standing in as pieces could easily have to make their way to their home base after dark.

Orin's theory proved correct. Outside, it didn't take long to find what we were looking for. One of the streetlights burned with a pale green light compared to the purple of the others. The house next to it was locked. The first house we'd found locked since starting the game.

"It's locked by magic," Orin said, pointing out that there was no keyhole. "I'm guessing it will only open to the playing pieces. It will have a memory charm on it."

I tried the handle again anyway, but it wouldn't budge.

"You'll not get past a spell like that," Orin said, but I paid no attention. I had another plan. Pulling off my jacket, I wrapped it around my hand and punched through the house's ground floor window. I'd always wanted to do that. I shook the jacket to clear the shards of broken glass before putting it back on and reaching through the hole I'd just made to unlock it.

"I guess they forgot to put a spell on the windows," I said, a grin playing on my lips as I slid the window up. Orin, looking suitably impressed, helped me climb up into the now open window.

Inside, the house was fancy and posh. It was a similar size to the faerie houses we'd already been inside, but it had been newly decorated to the highest degree. Sleek modern furniture filled the small living area, and I could just make out the ultra-modern kitchen through a door, all white granite and subway tile.

Orin pointed to the stairs, and I nodded. We tiptoed up slowly, although if he hadn't heard the breaking glass, he was hardly going to hear our footsteps. He was probably sleeping off the effects of the whiskey he'd no doubt been consuming all day.

We found Niall in the bedroom in an oversized bed. The pillows had been pushed to the floor, and the thick duvet only partially covered him. Everything from the back of his thighs upwards was completely naked. I heaved a sigh of relief he was sleeping on his stomach. Though I didn't particularly need the image of his flabby bum burned in my memory, either.

"Oy, Niall!" Orin shouted, making me jump.

"Hmmm?"

Niall turned to face us, and apart from a momentary expression of surprise, he didn't seem too bothered that we'd barged in on him while he was sleeping. I turned, fixing my eyes on the corner of the room.

"I wondered when you'd be back," Niall drawled, wiping the sleep from his eyes. "Want some chess advice, do you?"

"Can you please cover yourself," I asked, indicating his

mostly naked body. I wasn't going to be able to concentrate on anything with *that* staring at me.

He pulled the duvet to his waist without the slightest hint of embarrassment. At least, one of us wasn't embarrassed. I could feel my cheeks flaming red.

"Sorry. What is it you want? If you're here to move me, you'll have to wait a few minutes while I have a drink."

Orin shook his head. "We are not here to move you, Niall."

"No," I added. "It's time you told us everything you know."

22

I t took a few minutes of cajoling to get Niall out of bed and into some pants. The promise of an Irish coffee was what did it in the end, and so Orin and I trudged downstairs to make good on our deal while Niall made himself...presentable-ish.

"What if he doesn't cooperate?" I whispered to Orin as I filled the coffee pot with water. "Can you handle him? Magically?"

Orin frowned, fumbling with a coffee filter as if he was seeing the foreign object for the first time. "Never made coffee before?" I asked bemused.

"Faeries are more...tea people."

"Of course, you are." I grabbed the filters from him and freed one, taking over.

"I think I can handle him if I plan ahead." Orin stroked his jaw, considering. "I'll put a spell on the coffee. Neutralizing his magic for a time. He'll never see it coming."

"Perfect. That should give us enough time—"

A cleared throat sounded behind us, and I turned with a

wide fake smile, praying Niall hadn't heard Orin's earlier sentence.

"Almost ready," I said. "Why don't you have a seat?"

Niall slid onto one of the stools on the other side of the kitchen island, rubbing his face with his hands.

"Nice place they put you up in here," I said.

"Perks of the job," Niall replied.

"Funny, the only perk my mother had was almost getting eaten by a pack of hellhounds." My tone had darkened considerably.

"Jacq, be nice," Orin cautioned.

"Had?" Niall asked. "She off the board?"

I nodded stiffly.

"Not good, them taking your queen this early. Doesn't bode well."

"Well, there have been some extenuating circumstances," I said through gritted teeth. The last thing I needed right now was a lecture about my shitty chess playing.

"Why don't you start with this while the coffee brews," Orin said, shoving a coffee mug that smelled of whiskey across the island. I raised an eyebrow at him, and he nodded infinitesimally.

Niall took a sip and closed his eyes in rapture. The man had a serious problem. Or two serious problems. Because now, his magic was spelled, and we could talk freely.

"We're not here to ask you about chess tactics," I said. "We're here to find out everything you know about the Brotherhood."

Niall looked up at that, his eyes shrewd. He looked around slowly. "Where's your camera gal? The redhead?"

"Sleeping," Orin said simply.

Niall nodded, looking into the mug. And then bolted for the door, his stool clattering to the ground behind him.

Orin and I lunged into action once we shook off our surprise, running after him.

Niall had made it halfway across the living room toward the front door when I tackled him to the ground, my arms around his waist. We both went down hard, the wind whooshing from my lungs.

Orin pulled a chair out from the nearby dining room table and hauled a stunned Niall up into it. He waved his hands over the man, securing his wrists and ankles to the chair. Niall shook his head slowly. "What'd you do to me? My magic?" he looked up accusingly at Orin. "Where is it?"

"Just a precaution," Orin said. "A required one, it seems. I'll give you your magic when you tell us everything you know."

I scrambled to my feet, adjusting my jacket. "We know what the Faerie king is planning," I said. "Tell us where the final anchor point is."

"There's no way you can stop him," Niall replied, his eyes misty. "This has been in motion for decades. Since Obanstone took the throne. Do you really think that some useless college brats in Oregon 'discovered' the first open portal to Faerwild?" I could tell that he'd be using air quotes if he had use of his hands.

I frowned. The story of Faerwild's discovery was the stuff of legends. A group of undergrads in the Oregon mountains had been playing with spells, thinking themselves amateur magicians, and had opened a portal to Faerwild. A faerie had come out, announcing itself to the world.

"Are you saying the king planned to expose the existence of faeries to the human world...on purpose?" Orin asked.

"Oh, yes. We're all pieces on his gameboard. Me, even

you, Orin. You,"—he looked at me—"were unexpected. But you've danced to his tune, nonetheless."

"What do you mean, me?" Orin asked, narrowing his dark eyes.

"Do you think it's a coincidence you're in this race? That you were that much better than the competition at auditions? You brought nothing special to the table. You were passable at best. But it never sat well with the king that your parents sent you away in defiance of him. He had hoped you would share your mother's gift for glamours. The race was his way of getting back at them, showing them that they could defy him for a time, but he was always in control. You may not belong to him like they do, but you dance for him, just the same."

Orin took a step back. "My parents didn't send me away. The king did."

I looked between Orin and Niall, bewildered. Orin's childhood had been hell after the king had banished him from the palace as a baby. It couldn't be true that Orin's parents had been the ones who had subjected him to all of that?

Niall shook his head at him sadly. "They thought you'd be safer, far away. They didn't realize how hard it can be for a little faerie alone in this cruel world."

"You're lying," Orin spat at him, taking a menacing step forward.

I stepped in hastily, laying a soft hand on his arm. "Let's not let him distract us," I said softly. "He's probably full of shit. We need to stay focused."

Orin's muscles were taut with tension under my hand, but after a moment, he relaxed, taking a step back. "You're right."

"Tell us where the anchor is," I said. "And we'll let you go."

Niall shook his head. "I won't."

Before I knew what I was doing, I stepped forward and punched him in the stomach with all my might.

He collapsed around my fist as much as he could, tied to the chair, a wheezing sound escaping him. "Tell us!" I cried. I didn't think I was much of a torturer, but Niall didn't seem very tough, either. Perhaps we could soften his resolve.

I stepped back, and to my surprise, when he looked up, he was laughing, his eyes sharp. I can't believe I ever thought he was harmless. "I've been...watching the board," he wheezed. "You're one move away from this all coming crashing down. Losing. Failing. Orin, your parents will be trapped. The two of you will never see each other again. But I can help you. I'll tell you what moves to make to win."

I felt the blood drain from me. My play had been erratic, what with all the stuff chasing us, and our pieces' shields failing. I turned to Orin. "The board."

Orin grabbed his pack where he'd stashed the board, and we pulled it out, setting it on the kitchen counter. We studied it, our backs turned to Niall. I didn't want to see his smug face if he was right.

And right he was. I realized with dismay what we'd done. They were within one move of checkmate. The only way we could stop it was by moving our bishop. Sacrificing Niall. And he was our only chance for the information on the final anchor point. I said as much to Orin in a low tone.

I heard Niall chuckling quietly over my shoulder, and my hands balled into fists. Damn, I wanted to punch him again. But I restrained myself, instead, looking up at Orin.

"We need the information," I said quietly. "We need to protect Niall. We need more time with him. To break him."

"What are you asking, Jacq?" Orin asked. "If we let them take our king, the game will be over. Niall will be pulled out of here anyway. So will we. We agreed, we have to keep this going. Until we can find the anchor."

"He's our only shot at the anchor. We'll take him with us to Cass and the ICCF. They'll know how to get the information from him."

"And what, we just...sacrifice my father?" Orin asked, taking a step back from me.

I chewed my lip. If there was another way, I couldn't see one. "You know I don't want to do that, but this is bigger than any one faerie or human. We need to stop the king. That has to be our top priority. Before...everything else," I said softly. I tried to take his hands, but he pulled them back from me, his face gone hard.

"Would you say that if it was your mother we'd have to sacrifice?"

"That's different, Orin," I said, putting my hands on my hips. "She's an innocent human. She knows nothing about this. Your father...he's in it. He decided to help. He knows how important this is."

"So he's a worthy sacrifice?" Orin shot back.

"Tick-tock," Niall said. Our whispered discussion had escalated to a full-blown argument.

"Shut up," Orin and I both yelled at Niall.

I blew out a breath, struggling to control my rising panic. The sun would be rising soon. We didn't have much time until our next move. I needed Orin onboard. Keeping Niall had to be our priority.

"We'll find another way," Orin said. "Please Jacq. I just got him back. Don't ask me to sacrifice him."

I felt awful. Could I really be asking Orin to give up his father? "I just got Cass back, too. And I'm not going to let her down. Let down the entire human race. Don't ask that of me."

Orin pursed his lips, his dark eyes boring into me. I had grown so comfortable with Orin over these past weeks, I had forgotten how terrifyingly intense he could be when he turned that gaze on you. It was like being stared down by a dark avenging angel.

"He's a strong magician," I said weakly. "You said so yourself. He'll be able to defend against whoever Tristam and Sophia throw at him."

"And if he can't?"

We looked at each other, facing off, but stuck. There was no good answer. Either we kept the game going, protecting our king and sacrificing Niall, or we ended it, taking our one shot to foil the king, but leaving Orin's dad unprotected.

Niall smiled smugly from his spot tied to the chair. Suddenly, I realized there was a third way. If we got Niall to talk right fricking now, we could sacrifice him and keep the game going.

I strode across the room, wound back, and punched him across the jaw. Pain exploded in my hand, stealing my breath. I hissed with the pain, but I punched him again, this time nailing him across the eyebrow. "Tell us where it is!" I reared back again and punched him in the stomach.

"Jacq!" Orin stepped forward and snaked his hands across my middle, hauling me back. I struggled against him, lunging for Niall once again. "Let me go! Tell us, you bastard!" I said, my arms flailing, reaching for Niall, wanting to punch and claw until he told us what we wanted to know.

"Jacq, stop!" Orin spun me, pushing me back toward the hallway. I stumbled to get my footing, starting back towards Niall. Orin's strong arms stopped me again. "He can't tell us anything if you knock him unconscious." He seized my shoulders and held me as I struggled. Finally, captive in his grip, I stilled, my chest heaving with the effort, my mind spinning in circles.

"Why don't you go outside for a few," he said, steering me for the back door. "Get some air."

23

I hated the woman I'd just become. Weeks of mental, emotional, and physical exhaustion had left me angry and raw. Angry enough to hurt someone who was tied up to a chair and defenseless. I told myself that it was for the greater good, that in hurting Niall, I was saving people's lives, but I'm not sure I even believed myself. The truth was, I just wanted to hit something.

The streetlights had now gone off as the light began to creep over the horizon. If we didn't make a decision soon, it would be made for us. The FFR or the king would figure out where we were if they didn't already know. We'd done our best to creep here through the streets, but the truth was, eyes were everywhere and nowhere was private.

I sucked in a deep breath, trying to quiet the turmoil in my head. When had this all become so hard? I was supposed to run through different terrains, dodging obstacles—not deciding who to save and who to sacrifice.

Orin had been right to send me outside to calm down. If I hadn't, my head would probably have exploded, but that didn't mean he was right about everything. I didn't want his dad to get hurt any more than I wanted anyone to get hurt, but Niall was the only person I could think of who could tell us the location of the last anchor. Without that information, Orin's father would be in just as big a mess as the rest of us. At worst, he'd only have to fight one of the other team's playing pieces. I'd seen his magic. He had a fighting chance. He was nothing like my mom, who knew nothing of magic or the ways of the fae.

I spun around on the spot for a minute as I weighed the two options in my head. Neither was particularly palatable, but we had to figure something out before the king sent another round of killer bees or fuck-knew-what else to hurry us along. Stepping back into the house, I still didn't know what to do. But I had calmed down and was willing to talk it through.

My newfound Zen became a moot point when I realized...Orin was gone.

"Where is he?" I asked, looking around the room in a panic. "Orin?" I shouted. Maybe he'd gone upstairs or to the bathroom.

When I heard no reply, I turned to Niall. "What did you do?"

Niall grinned at me, the blue of a bruise just beginning to appear on his forehead, blood trickling from his split lip. "I think he got sick of you telling him what to do. He left out of the back door."

"You're lying," I protested. He couldn't have. Orin wouldn't have left me alone on this chessboard from hell. "You must have done something!"

Niall shook his head. "Notice I'm still tied up. What exactly do you think I could have done?"

It was a rhetorical question. There was nothing he could have done without his magic, and Orin had taken care of that. I dashed into the kitchen where the back door was located. It was wide open. I looked both ways down the back alley, but Orin was nowhere to be seen.

The weight of panic crushed my chest as I took in the enormity of what had just happened. I couldn't believe he'd just left me to do this alone.

I stepped back inside the kitchen, feeling the room growing small around me. I took a deep breath and then another, grabbing onto the countertop to steady myself.

When I pulled myself up straight, a piece of paper came away from the countertop stuck to my hand. I hadn't seen it at first as it was white—the same color as the granite countertop. On it was a hastily scribbled note in Orin's handwriting.

GONE *to move a piece and expose the king. I hope you are right about Niall. I found something in my backpack that might help you charm the bastard. Not that you needed any help charming me. See you soon.*

THE NOTE DIDN'T MEAN a lot of sense until I noticed the small vial he'd left on the countertop. My eyes widened as I recognized it.

It was the love potion given to him by the xana in the very first trial. I'd completely forgotten about it until now. I allowed a smile to play on my lips as I reread his words. It was so unlike Orin to flirt, but I found I liked it. And he'd chosen to try things my way and throw the game. I only hoped his father would be all right. I'd never forgive myself, otherwise.

If Orin was off to move our piece, it meant I didn't have much time until the game was over. Picking up the vial, I unscrewed the top. No point putting it in Niall's drink. He'd fallen for that trick once today, I doubted he was stupid enough to fall for it twice.

I strode into the living room and pushed his head back, plugging his nose. I poured the small potion down his throat. Thank god he was tied up or this would have been impossible.

"What the hell are you doing?" he gurgled as the green liquid dripped down his throat.

The potion worked like a charm because as soon as I stepped back, his face softened, turning from anger to something foreign. Adoration. I'd have laughed if it wasn't so serious.

"My gods, you're beautiful," he breathed, looking at me like I made the sun come up. "Have I ever told you that before?"

"Not to my knowledge," I replied, biting back a smile.

"Well, I was stupid and foolish not to have told you sooner. Your beauty surpasses all others."

I didn't know how long the potion would last, so I had to be quick.

"You're a handsome man too, but you know what really turns me on?" I suppressed a shudder even as I said the words. Me and Niall? Ew.

His eyes lit up, and he was practically dribbling. That xana magic was strong stuff.

"Tell me, my sweet."

"I like knowledge. I want to know where the final anchor is."

His mouth twisted and a furrow appeared on his forehead as he knotted his brows together. He was trying to fight the potion.

"Will it make you love me?" His words were lovely, his tone not.

"More than anything else," I encouraged.

"It's right in the center of the board where four squares meet. Two black and two white. You'll never find it, though. It's protected in ways you'll never discover."

"Can you tell me how?"

Niall's face contorted once again. "No," he spat, sweat beading his brow. He was really fighting it, overcoming it for a moment. "You have no idea what you're up against, and you can drug me all you want, but even I don't know everything. The king has his own enchantments all around the finish line."

But then he gasped, and his face contorted into pleading. "Please, darling, release me so I can show you how much you mean to me!" I ignored him, and I ran back into the kitchen and whipped out the two-way mirror that Cass had given me. *The finish line.* It was like we'd thought. The king wanted the race to end with a bang.

"Cass," I shouted into it, urging her to answer. I didn't know how much time I had left, and every second was precious.

"Jacq! Thank god, I've been worried sick. The FFR stopped broadcasting a few hours ago, and no one knows why. The whole of Faerwild is up in arms about it. It's so weird to see just how famous my own sister is. I was worried they'd captured you."

It was so good to hear her voice—like a rock in the ocean of madness. "We're still playing. But Orin's about to throw the game."

Cass's eyes widened. She turned her head to the side. "Guys, come here. Jacq's on the line. Orin's throwing the game."

Louis and Auberon came into view behind Cass. "Did you find the last anchor?" she asked me.

"Yeah, that's why I'm calling. It's in the center of the board. Right in the middle of the four squares. I don't know how you'll even get to it. It's protected too. Enchantments, I think, but I'm not sure."

"We'll figure it out. Great job, Jacq."

"Cass, it's the finish line of the race. Orin's dad told us that to blow the anchor points, the king needs human blood. I think the king plans to use Tristam's partner, Sophia, as a sacrifice."

Cass paled. "We'll get there first, Jacq. I swear."

"Jacq." Another voice lifted me from the mirror. Orin. He was back, and I'd never been more happy to see him.

"I moved a pawn," he said. "This is it. The game is over. Did you give the potion to Niall?"

I nodded my head. "Yes, the location is here on the board. I've just told Cass." I motioned to the mirror on the work surface. All it showed was the reflection of the ceiling. Cass and the others were gone.

Orin took my hand, and we stepped outside. It was over. The Fantastic Faerie Race was finished. In a matter of minutes, Tristam and Sophia would make their next move. They'd be the victors. I just prayed Orin's dad could protect himself.

Relief mixed with fear scrambled together to create a mixed bag of emotions. I didn't know what was going to happen next, but I did know that it was out of our hands. I had to trust Cass to find the anchor and dismantle the MEDs before the king sacrificed Sophia.

Orin pulled out the little game board and placed it in the countertop. We watched together as Tristam and Sophia's bishop moved into position.

Checkmate.

24

———

Orin and I stood there for a long moment. He put his arm around me, I leaned in to him. "Your dad will be okay," I said quietly. "If he's anything like you, he's a survivor."

"I know," Orin said, resting his chin on top of my head.

I was loathe to leave the moment, unsure of what we would face next, but I knew we couldn't stay here forever. "I guess we should go outside and wait for the producers to come pick us up?" I desperately hoped that's who would meet us, not the king's guards. I prayed the king would be too concerned with getting to the final anchor point and trying to blow up the Hedge to focus on two little race contestants.

It didn't feel right, standing here waiting while Cass and Auberon and the ICCF finished the battle. But that was crazy. We'd done our part. We'd found the anchor. We hadn't started this fight. It wasn't our job to end it. What could we do that trained agents from a powerful international organization couldn't do? I'd watched too many movies. I needed to leave it to the professionals.

Orin straightened, rubbing my back. "Let's go."

We passed Niall on our way out of the house. "Where are you going?" he howled at us. "You can't just leave me here! I'll die without you, my sweet butterfly!"

Butterfly? Orin mouthed at me.

I just shook my head.

"The magic will wear off in a few hours," Orin said. "You'll be fine, lover boy." Hopefully, the ICCF would have been successful by then, and they could come pick Niall up and throw him in prison.

Outside, the pale blue sky promised a beautiful day. I breathed in the fresh air. Either everything would be okay, or this might be my last morning of freedom. I didn't have it in me to worry. My well of emotions seemed to have run dry. All that was left was calm.

"Why are the squares still on the ground?" Orin asked. I frowned. He was right. The ground we were standing on was still painted that strange white.

"Let me see the board," I said. He handed it to me, and I held it out, both of us looking at it. All the pieces were still there. Not our king, but all the others.

"Why haven't they picked up any of the pieces?" I asked. "Why haven't they come for us? Isn't the race over?"

"Yeah." Orin put his hands on his hips. "Patricia should be shoving a microphone in our faces right now."

"Do you still have the original clue?" I asked.

Orin fished in the pocket of his jacket and pulled out the rumpled piece of paper. I scanned it again.

It's time to prove your mastery,
Of color and piece and square,
One at a time you'll find them,

Those you love so fair.
But if you are to end it,
You mustn't take the bait,
Across the board you'll soldier,
'Till king becomes your mate.

"It says if we are to end it, we have to make the king our mate," I mused.

"But Tristam and Sophia already did. They won."

"What if they won the game, but not the race? What if the game is just a way to get to the next checkpoint? Each of the trials had multiple legs," I pointed out.

Orin groaned. "Are you saying this thing isn't over?"

"Sure as hell doesn't seem like it's over, does it?"

"No," he admitted.

We crowded around the game board again. "Look, if we move Niall, we can take Gabe, their king."

"Ugh, I was hoping I'd never have to see him again."

"You think I want to go anywhere with that lovesick creep?"

"Just float to the next square, sweet butterfly," Orin said in a sing-song voice.

I punched him in the arm. Hard. "It's a powerful potion."

"It would have to be," Orin said. "I gave that xana quite a kiss."

I scoffed, rolling my eyes. "Ugh. Watching that kiss was—" I opened and shut my mouth, trying to find the right word.

"Pulse-pounding? Envy-inducing? Knee-melting?"

"Nauseating," I finished, crossing my arms before my chest.

"You were so jealous," Orin teased.

"I was not jealous!" I protested, but my voice went up about an octave, which didn't help make my comment any more convincing.

"You were positively green."

"Get over yourself, Casanova," I said. "Let's just get Niall to Gabe's square and be done with this."

"You know," Orin said, pulling me back against his chest as I started to walk inside the house. His lips lingered by my ear, his arm wrapped around my torso, pulling me against the hard plane of his chest. "When this is all over, I'm going to kiss you like that. Except my lips are going to explore every inch of your body."

Heat pooled inside me at his whispered promise, and I found myself leaning back into him, my eyes fluttering closed.

And then, he spun me around to face him, and my eyes popped open. "See!" he said with glee. "Jealous!"

He jogged back inside the house, leaving me, weak-kneed and flustered, to compose myself.

I struggled to glare at him as he returned with Niall at his side, but I couldn't fight the smile that wanted to break free. Even amidst the madness, danger, and death, Orin could make me laugh. I wouldn't forget it.

"Rule Number One," I said to Niall, pulling him up as he tried to go to one knee before me. "If you want to win my love, you need to be quiet. No professions of love. Rule number two. Do exactly as I say. Got it?"

He nodded, wide-eyed, his hands reaching out to grab one of mine.

"Rule number three," I said. "Don't touch me. Let's go."

We strode across the game board, through square after square. I was exhausted and hungry, but adrenaline pushed me forward relentlessly. We were so close. I could feel it. We would do this.

As we reached Gabe's square, the sun was bright in the sky. There should be birds chirping, but the city around us was silent. "He's close," I said. "Now Niall—"

But we turned a corner and Gabe was there. Before I could instruct Niall, he threw out a hand, and a jet of blue magic slammed into Gabe, who was thrown off his feet, tumbling into the cobblestone street, where he rolled to a stop.

"Niall!" I shrieked, and Orin and I ran forwards, to Gabe's side. I'd seen the purple shield flash around Gabe as Niall's magic had hit him, so hopefully, he wasn't too badly wounded.

Gabe groaned and rolled to the side, pushing himself up to a seated position.

"Are you all right?" I asked. As I knelt, I realized the black ground beneath me had transformed into regular gray stone. The board had disappeared. By taking the king, we'd finished the game.

He shook his head and grunted, before holding out a hand to Orin. Orin grabbed him and helped him stand. "I'm alive. Gonna need to ask for hazard pay for this."

"Do you think we could get that?" I asked, hopefully.

Gabe gave a little laugh, shaking his head, blinking. He finally focused on us, then on Niall behind us. "I'd say it's good to see you again, but..."

"Do you want me to hit him again?" Niall asked, holding out his hands.

"No," I said. "Just...stand over there." I hadn't even known Niall had his magic back. I guess what Orin gave him had worn off. Good thing the xana's spell hadn't.

Gabe raised his eyebrow at my instructions to Niall, but I just shook my head. "It's a long story."

"All right. Well, congrats you two. You've completed the game and earned your next clue."

Orin and I looked at each other with dismay. "We were afraid you were going to say that."

Gabe pulled an envelope out of his pocket, dusting it off. "This is the last one. Solve this clue and find your way to the final checkpoint. The end of the race. If you're still here, it looks like Tristam and Sophia haven't won yet."

"Give it here," I said, my competitive urge kicking back in. I'd been so focused on finding the anchor point and staying alive, I'd forgotten about the race. Winning hadn't seemed important. But now...we had a chance to win it all. And Niall had confirmed that the final anchor point was the end of the race. If we got there first...maybe we could help save Sophia—and the world in the process.

Gabe handed over the clue, and I ripped into it.

You'll find the finish line
  Inside a place divine
  Now's not the time to falter
  The end's at the scarlet altar

Orin looked up. "The Temple of Titania."

"What?" I asked.

"It's a temple. In the middle of the old town. It's a place divine, and it's known for its altar covered in garnets, so it looks like blood."

"You faeries are weird as hell," I said. "But it fits what Niall told us. Let's go."

I wasn't sure what to do with Niall, but when I turned to tell him to scurry off, he'd already disappeared.

"Where…" I trailed off, suddenly uneasy. Why had he left? Maybe the xana's potion had finally worn off?

"Clock is ticking," Gabe said, shooing us in the direction of the temple. "Go!"

25

———

There was something nice about it just being the two of us again. All through the race, there had been other people along for the ride. Other teams, camera people, those trying to kill or eat us, not to mention the millions of people watching us from the comfort of their own homes. With Ruth still absent, it was only Orin and I running through the town, weaving our way through the quaint little backstreets, passing houses and shops that all looked almost mundane now that the chessboard spell had worn off. As if anything in Faerwild could ever be mundane.

"There," Orin said, pointing to a spire in the distance. I drew in my breath as the ivory temple came into view, its four magnificent golden domes reflecting the sun's rays. I couldn't believe I'd missed the temple—it dominated the skyline almost as much as the palace spires, and could be seen from a great distance. I guess I'd been focused on other things. You know, like not dying, keeping my mother from dying, keeping all of humanity from perpetual enslavement.

"Hang on," I panted, asking Orin to stop.

"What's up? We need to hurry."

"I know, but...it's important. Can I look at the board again?"

Orin shrugged and unshouldered his backpack. Opening it, he passed me the board. The playing pieces had all disappeared. Whether it meant they were all off the board in real life or it was just that the magic had faded now that the game was over, I didn't know.

"What are you looking for?" Orin queried, looking over my shoulder at the board.

"I wanted to see if we were heading to the middle of the board where the anchor is. But if we're here," I pointed to the board where a tiny temple showed, "then we're far enough away not to worry."

Orin took the board from me and placed it back in his bag. "We thought the finish line would be at the anchor point, but maybe we were wrong. Maybe the king plans to sacrifice some other human. Because I'm sure the Temple of Titania is where the clue is leading us."

"Agreed."

He placed his hands on my face, gently caressing my cheekbone with one thumb. "Soon, we'll be able to walk away from this madness. Go back to our normal lives. We'll win the race, and Cass and the others will dismantle any MED that was placed around the anchor."

I hoped he was right.

He took my hand, and we once again set off toward the temple. It was okay for him to say that we were close to returning to our normal lives, but I knew for sure my life would never be normal again. I'd seen too much, done too much. I could never go back to fetching coffee for John or being a gopher in a studio. Nor did I want the fame that was sure to dog us when the race was over. Then, there was the small matter of how Orin and I would stay together. It's not like we could commute from Faerwild to Earth. And so... where would we live? I couldn't imagine my life without Orin now, but I also couldn't see where I'd fit in Faerwild. And Orin was so different; would he ever feel at home on Earth? Among humans? Wherever we lived, one of us was sure to be an outcast.

I threw the thoughts to one side as we began to pick up speed again. The temple was even more magnificent close-up. The white facade was decorated with intricate sculptures of strange faerie creatures, and as we passed beneath a delicate arch that held the two carved front doors, I couldn't help but look up and goggle at the craftsmanship.

As we stepped inside the temple's interior, the beauty of the space took my breath away. I wasn't religious, but at that moment, the hair rose on the back of my neck—I felt something...spiritual. The high vaulted ceilings echoed our footsteps as we walked hand in hand past the pews to the altar. Orin had been right. It was literally covered in garnets that sparkled in such a way that gave the appearance of blood seeping right from the altar itself.

"Close, but no cigar." A voice came from the other side of the vast altar, and my heart fell into my shoes as I recognized whom it belonged to.

"Shit!" I whispered under my breath as Tristam and Sophia stepped out into our line of sight.

"Nice to see you too," Sophia huffed, sarcastically.

"What now?" I asked, looking around. As far as I could see, we were the only four in the whole temple. They'd shaken off their cameraperson, too, it seemed. If this was the end of the race, it was highly anti-climactic.

"Actually, we thought you might know."

Orin let out a laugh, which bounced off the walls and reverberated back to us. I shivered as the laugh multiplied, turning into a thunderous boom. That, coupled with the blood-like appearance of the altar, turned my sense of awe to one of foreboding. There should have been an endpoint here. Cameras. Confetti. A big ribbon to run through. Something to mark the finish of the race. But instead, there were only the four of us and the vast space around us.

"You don't know?" Orin said. "We've come all this way, and that's it? All this for a tie?"

"It's not a tie," argued Tristam. "No one has crossed the finish line yet."

"So where is the finish line?" Orin asked. "The clue was pretty clear. The end is at the scarlet altar. Unless you know of any other scarlet altars near here?"

Tristam shook his head while Sophia pouted next to him.

There not being a finish line here bothered me a lot more than not being able to end the race. Something wasn't right, and yet again, I was left with the feeling that we were all being tricked. But why trick Tristam? It made no sense. The king wanted him to win, and yet, it appeared Tristam was no closer to solving the problem than we were.

I moved forward to get a better look at the altar to see if another clue had been left for us. The altar was an ornate stone rectangle about as high as my shoulders, but it was wider than any I'd ever seen in the human world. Not that I'd seen many, but this one was at least as large as a king-sized bed. What exactly they used it for, I didn't want to know. Images of human sacrifices filled my mind as I leaped up onto the top to take a closer look at the carvings decorating the surface.

Almost as soon as I'd hauled myself up, the floor beneath my feet began to rumble. My first thought was that the FFR was playing with us, and this was another trial. We hadn't had to deal with an earthquake yet, but it seemed to be only me that it was affecting. I was falling...no, not falling, I was being lowered as the top of the altar sank inside the walls of it.

When the others noticed what was happening, they scrambled to jump over the walls of the altar. Tristam and Orin managed it easily, but Sophia in the short skirt she'd elected to wear instead of her FFR uniform had more trouble. We were already below floor level as she reached the top of the altar walls and peered down at us as we descended lower still.

"Make it stop!" she cried out.

Tristam held his hands up in the air. "I can't. You're going to have to jump. I'll try to cushion your landing with air."

We were about ten feet lower than her now, and I didn't expect her to do it, but the lure of a million dollars must have been too much. She launched herself down, landing partly in Tristam's arms and partly on the altar top with a thud.

"Fuck!" she hissed, her face contorted with pain. "I think it's broken. I thought you were going to catch me!"

"Sorry." Tristam's face reddened. "I didn't get my magic ready in time. Next time give me some warning."

"So this is my fault?" she scoffed.

A better person would have felt sorry for her, but the thought running through my head was that we'd easily beat them now. If Sophia couldn't walk, they couldn't cross the finish line.

"Can you stand on it?" Tristam asked through gritted teeth. He was obviously having the same thought I was.

Even if he carried her, he wouldn't be able to race as quickly as Orin and I.

"Yes, I think so."

"Then it's not broken. You probably just sprained it."

"I'll use magic to brace it," she said, trying to put on a brave face. But we all knew that even if she did, she still wouldn't be able to run as fast as I.

My glee was short-lived as the altar top hit the ground with a thump. We must have been thirty feet underground by this point. The rectangular shaft of light beaming from above our heads was the only illumination of the space we found ourselves in, which looked to be some sort of carved tunnel. Please not another goblin mine!

"Come on," I said, grabbing Orin's hand and setting off into the dark tunnel ahead of us. As we moved into the stone tunnel, I spotted stone coffins laid into recesses in the wall. So not a goblin mine. We were in a crypt. The place where they buried their dead. Another shiver passed through me at the thought of it. I'm not sure which was worse.

"Wait." Orin pulled on my hand, bringing me to a standstill. Behind us, Tristam was struggling to help Sophia walk.

I looked at Orin, already knowing what he was thinking. "You can't be serious after everything they've done."

"We can still cross the line first," he reasoned. "But we don't know how long this passage goes on and we can't leave them like that. She's in pain. She needs a doctor."

"You're worried about Sophia?" I looked at him like he had grown a second head. "When I first met you, I thought you were a selfish bastard and look at you now. I've ruined you," I said, with a little spark of pride.

"Yes, I'm worried about Sophia," he huffed. "But you can hold the Nobel Peace Prize. We don't know where this tunnel goes, or what we'll find at the end. If it happens to be something unfriendly, we'll stand a better chance against it with Tristam and Sophia there."

"There's the old Orin I know and love," I said. Though I found it didn't bother me much anymore. It was just part of who he was. Faeries growing up on their own in this cruel world didn't have the luxury of kindness. Anyway, he was right. I wouldn't put it past the FFR to position some final boss monster right before the finish line.

"Yeah, sweetness and light," he growled. "Come on."

We walked back to the struggling pair. Orin picked up Sophia in his arms and began to walk into the dark. Tristam didn't look particularly happy about the situation, but he accepted our strange kindness. He knew he couldn't cross the finish line without Sophia, and he couldn't carry her quickly enough to beat us.

The walk through the underground tunnel was slow going. The paving stones were uneven, making the walk difficult, and the lack of light did nothing to help. The farther we walked from the alter top, the darker it was, and before long, we were having to feel our way rather than see.

"Can one of you conjure up a magical light?" I huffed as I stubbed my toe on an uneven stone.

"Don't waste your magic on my account," a voice boomed through the tunnel. A green flash lit up the room and fizzed out, but not before I saw who'd conjured the magic. My pulse rapidly increased as I prayed I was wrong, but then the whole place lit up in a brilliant white light. I squinted against the glare, blinking.

Standing in a large vaulted chamber was Vale Obanstone. Behind him with a leering grin on her face was Patricia, and behind her, the end of the race. I got ready to bolt for the finish line when something else caught my eye, and I froze.

The king and Patricia stood before a set of stairs leading up to a stone platform. From the platform—an altar of sorts

—sprouted a large obelisk that flashed with rivers of lavender light pulsing through cut out channels. At the base was something that looked suspiciously like a bomb. And in Patricia's manicured hand was a sleek silver pistol.

It was as we'd feared. This wasn't the finish line. This was the final anchor point and the culmination of the Brotherhood's mad plan.

26

"What is this?" Tristam said, looking around in confusion. "Where's the finish line? Where are the cameras?"

Orin put Sophia down, and she hopped to Tristam's side, hissing with each step.

"There is no finish line," I said, proud that I managed to keep my voice from wavering. "Is there."

Patricia raised the pistol and pointed it at Orin and me.

"Not for you, I'm afraid," King Obanstone said. "But for me, for the Brotherhood, we are finally at the end of a race we have run for a very long time."

"The Brotherhood?" Tristam asked, shooting a worried glance at me. "Father, what do you have to do with those terrorists?"

"Tristam, what's going on?" Sophia asked quietly.

I told you so! I wanted to shout at them.

"The Brotherhood are not terrorists," Patricia said, stepping forward. She wore a long black dress that looked suspiciously like a robe. Apparently, she'd cast aside her "TV show host" wardrobe for full villain attire. "The ICCF are the terrorists. Ripping apart the natural world, forcing us to separate into humans and faeries. But that's not how it's supposed to be. We're just returning the world to the way it was intended." I really didn't like how the pistol barrel wavered whenever she tried to emphasize a point. She didn't look like a pro with that thing. I didn't want it to accidentally go off.

"I thought the final anchor point was supposed to be in the middle of the board," Orin whispered to me. "Why the hell is it here?"

The king must have heard him because he leered at Orin. "Didn't anyone tell you not to trust a drunk?"

I opened and closed my mouth, the pieces slotting into place. "Niall was a plant. Misdirection."

"Well, he told a partial truth," Patricia said gleefully. "We couldn't be sure what kind of spell you would use on him to get him to talk. The final anchor is at the very center of the board." She waved her hands around the ancient chamber as if on a game show. "Just about half a mile underground."

Shit. That meant Cass and Auberon and the rest were... way too far away to help us. They'd be looking on the surface, and find a big ol' bag of nothing.

"Father," Tristam insisted, not willing to have the attention off him for even a second. "What is going on here?"

"Let me tell you, my dear boy." Vale strode down the stairs and ushered Tristam and a limping Sophia towards the anchor point.

My mind was whirling at this point. We needed to get the MED away from that magical anchor. But there was no way Orin and I could do it alone. We needed backup. We needed Cass. Even if we could escape from here unscathed, we didn't have enough time to get out of here, find them, and get back before the king blew the whole Hedge. But maybe I could alert her...

The king was gesturing wildly now at the huge obelisk, explaining the division of the worlds, the Brotherhood's mission, the race.

"So the race was just...a distraction?" Sophia asked dismayed. "Was there ever a million dollar prize? A boon?" I could tell she was devastated that she'd put herself through hell for nothing when she could have been on a beach in Ibiza the whole time.

I crept my hand into my pocket, grasping for Cass's mirror. "Cass," I whispered, praying it was loud enough to trigger the mirror's connection.

"Father," Tristam said. "I don't think this is a good idea. Maybe once upon a time, the worlds were joined, but it's been different for millennia. Technology can't exist around quora. You'd topple the human world, their financial markets, governments. I can't imagine that's what you want..." he trailed off as he saw the gleam in his father's eyes. Tristam took a step back, paling. "That *is* what you want."

The mirror was in my hand now, and I flicked it open, still inside my jacket pocket.

The king continued. "The faerie races are vastly superior to humans. It's wrong that we scrape for resources while humans flourish, taking the best of this planet—"

"Jacq? Jacq, are you there?" Cass's voice crackled out of the mirror, and my stomach squeezed like a vice. I clapped the mirror closed, but it was too late.

The king and Patricia whirled towards me, Patricia's pistol trained on me, the king's hands raised. "What was that?"

"What was what?" I asked weakly.

Patricia strode to me, her heels clicking on the stones. She pointed the gun at my temple, pressing the cool barrel against my skin.

"Easy!" Orin said, but the king turned to him.

"Don't you move."

"Give. It. Here," Patricia said to me, her voice cold as ice.

I swallowed and offered the mirror. *Idiot. Idiot, Idiot!* She took it from me, backing away with her gun still trained on Orin and me. I swallowed, my heart stuttering.

She handed the king the mirror, and he flipped it open. He sneered as a face came into view.

"Cassandra Cunningham. No doubt the ICCF rabble is with you, searching helplessly for an MED you'll never find. What's the human expression? Always a day late and a dollar short." He snorted.

"Father," another voice stemmed from the mirror. "Don't do—" but it was cut off as the king dropped the mirror to the ground and crushed it with a savage stomp of his boot.

"Who was that?" Tristam asked, his voice wavering. "Father, that sounded like—"

"I told you your brother was alive," I said, realizing that if we could get Tristam and Sophia on our side, we were four against two. Well, Sophia was kind of worthless, so maybe like three and a half against two. "Your father's been lying to you this whole time. Your brother fled because your father was going to kill him for discovering his twisted secret!"

The king's face contorted with rage. He crossed the chamber faster than my eyes could take in and backhanded me across the face. Stars exploded in my vision, and I hit the ground hard.

"Don't touch her!" Orin shouted, shooting a jet of purple

flame at the king. The king deflected it easily, and a shot rang out.

I jerked up, my eyes searching Orin's body for any sign he'd been hit. There was none. Patricia had fired her gun in the air. "Nobody move until I say," she said, her normally chipper voice low and deadly.

"Orin, Jacq, get over here." She gestured towards the obelisk, and we obeyed. My cheekbone smarted like hell where the king had slapped me. Damn, the man hit hard.

"Tristam, tie them up," the king retrieved a coil of black rope and tossed it to his son. Tristam caught it with a face like he'd just been thrown a poisonous viper. "Father—"

"Do it!" the king barked.

Tristam stumbled forward and faced us, unable to look us in the eyes. "Turn around and hold out your hands," he mumbled. I glowered at him, wanting to scream at him. But something held me back, some glimmer of sanity through my anger. Tristam was our only chance at getting out of this mess. "It's not too late to do the right thing," I murmured under my breath. "Auberon made the right choice. You can too."

"Silence," the king commanded.

I pressed my lips shut. I wasn't sure if my words had gotten through to Tristam, but I had to hope that there was something good inside him. Something that knew this was wrong. Some part that was brave enough to stand up to his father.

When Tristam had tied our hands securely, he stepped back, and the king stepped forward, any sign of rage gone, replaced by his normal, calm, regal appearance. "You two will be the first tragic victims of an awful ICCF mistake. Technology designed to keep everyone safe will, well, be the end of life as you know it."

"You're going to try to pin this on the ICCF? No one will buy that."

"They will when I'm done with it. Without television or the internet, it will be a simple matter of spreading the story I want and squashing the rest." The king stepped in close and seized my chin.

"You Cunninghams have been a thorn in my side ever since your worthless sister took my son from me. You'll be a fitting sacrifice to bring an end to the world as we know it. It's almost poetic."

"I hate poems," I spat at him, through that wasn't entirely true. When Orin had recited that van Goethe poem about the Erl-King during the Sorcery Trial, it had a nice lilt to it...

The king seized my arm and pulled me forward, up the stairs to the raised platform where the base of the obelisk sat.

Orin started after us, but Patricia trained her weapon on him. "Ah-ah-ahh, handsome," she said. "Don't you move. Or you'll be next."

The king threw me forward to my knees, and I hit the ground hard. A sleek silver box with a blinking red timer faced me. But I wouldn't have time to worry about that. Because I'd already be dead by the time it went off.

27

———

"I think you already know what's going to happen next, don't you?" the king sneered.

I remained still, not giving him the satisfaction of an answer. If he wanted to give me a whole bad guy monologue about how amazing he was and what he was going to do, so be it. But I wasn't going to have any part of it.

He whipped out a curved dagger and held my face up so I could get a good look at the weapon that was going to kill me.

"Pretty isn't it? You know, this has been in my family for generations. I was going to give it to Auberon, but once I'm gone, it will pass to Tristam."

"Sooner rather than later," I spat, turning my eyes away from the sharp blade. At least it would go in easily and, hopefully, lessen the pain. I frantically tried to think of anything else we had up our sleeve, but we'd used the xana potion, and my mirror was crushed into shards and scattered all over the floor. If my arms weren't tied behind my back at the wrists, I'd have gone for one of the shards to even up the playing field a little, but as it was, I was out of options.

"With your lifeblood spilled onto the foundation of the altar, there will be enough magical power to obliterate the vile Hedge that has divided the natural world. Your sacrifice will not be in vain. You will be a part of ushering in a glorious new era for all faerie-kind."

He pulled the dagger away quickly, so now all I could see was the floor. I twisted my head so I was looking straight at Orin. There was so much I wanted to say to him, so many things I wished I'd told him, but it was too late. I could already feel the point of the dagger in my side, ripping through the fabric of the FFR uniform.

I love you, I mouthed to him soundlessly. What else was there to say? I would be dead within the minute and telling him I loved him was the best I could do.

I'd seen Orin at some pretty low points, but I'd never seen tears flowing down his face the way they were now. He was so angry, and my whispered proclamation of love only served to make him angrier still. Patricia had tied his legs too, and now he thrashed on his side, kicking and writhing to free himself of the rope. It was a valiant effort, but it would be too late. He'd never get to me in time, and even if he did, they'd only kill him too.

"Stop!" A voice called out.

I felt a sharp pain in my side as I was dragged roughly away, scraping my cheek along the cold stone floor. My ropes loosened, and I found I could move again. Pulling myself up, I saw it was Tristam that had saved me. He'd pulled me away from his father. It was him I'd heard yelling stop.

Blood dripped down my side, staining the uniform below the rip, but it was a shallow cut, barely breaking the skin. Tristam had pulled me away before his father could cause too much damage.

"This is madness, Father," Tristam said. "You can't do this. You can't just... kill people. And you?" Tristam pointed to Patricia. "How do you think this will go for humans when the Hedge goes down? Why are you even helping him?"

I took advantage of Tristam's distraction to scramble over to Orin and began to work on his ropes. Mine had been cut, whether with a knife or with magic, I didn't know, but I had neither of those to aid me now. I only had my fingers and a few years in Girl Scouts on my side.

"Patricia grew up in the Brotherhood," the king said smoothly. "Her father was one of our most esteemed members. Everything she has is thanks to our efforts. She knows there is always a place for those who are loyal. Unlike you, who are being dangerously disloyal. Cease this prattling, son. The human must die."

I looked up sharply at that, just in time to see Tristam barrel into his father like a linebacker. The king took a shoulder to the gut, apparently not expecting a physical attack. I ignored the commotion, intent on getting Orin free. It was only when a scream rang out, echoing throughout the chamber that I finally looked up.

Somehow, the king had gotten Tristam off him. Now Sophia was struggling in the king's arms, and Tristam was watching helplessly as Patricia held a gun on him.

"Get off me, you asshole!" Sophia cried.

I had to give it to her. Sophia was putting up a good fight. But the king was stronger.

"One of these humans has to die, my boy," the king said. "Their blood is all the same. If you want to save the blonde one, you leave me no choice."

Then everything happened at once. Sophia bit down

into the king's hand, causing him to drop her to the floor. They both screamed in pain at the same time; Vale, because of his hand, and Sophia because she'd landed on her ankle. Tristam ran towards her to pull her away at the exact moment I finally loosened Orin's ropes enough for him to escape.

"Just do it already!" Patricia screamed amidst all the chaos. A shot rang out, deafening in the echoing chamber. I held my hands to my ears as everything played out as if in slow motion. I looked frantically at Orin, but he appeared fine.

It seemed that nobody moved for a couple of seconds, but then Sophia's eyes widened. A bloom of red spread out from a wound in her shoulder. Patricia's bullet had struck her. She moaned, crumpling in on herself.

"No!" Somebody screamed out as Sophia began to fall to the floor. It could have been me, it could have been Orin or Tristam. Perhaps it was all three of us. Tristam caught her, lowering her to the floor.

The king moved quickly and backhanded Tristam across the face, knocking him away from Sophia. I winced, as I had just felt the force of such a blow a few minutes ago myself. It seemed it was the king's go-to move. "We need her lifeblood spilled on the foundation!" The king said, beginning to drag her towards the huge obelisk.

Sophia screamed in agony as he wrenched her arm attached to her wounded shoulder. "Help me, Patricia," he cried. He was just steps from the obelisk. And Sophia's blood was all he needed to detonate the MED and take out the final anchor.

Tristam was back on his feet and exploded at his father with a howl, knocking the king back with a right hook to the jaw.

I was impressed, but there wasn't any time. "Patricia," Orin cried, as the TV host in heels had taken the king's place dragging Sophia.

We pounded up the stairs to the altar, but she saw us and seized her pistol from the dusty floor, aiming wild shots at us. As her pistol swung towards me, a bullet hit something in front of us and harmlessly fell to the floor. A sheen of purple light illuminated the space between Patricia and us. Orin had produced a force field that had saved us. We took advantage of the protection to scramble to the side, behind an ancient stone statue that flanked the staircase.

Patricia kept firing, and her bullets hit the ceiling and the wall. But that didn't mean she couldn't get lucky.

I risked a peek out from behind the statue and Patricia got off another shot. This one whizzed just inches from my head, taking a chunk of stone with it. She fired again, sending another loud bang ringing through my ears followed by the clink of metal on stone. She fired again, and I heard the click of the cartridge. She was empty.

As we stood Patricia stalked towards us with a sneer on her face. This was not the face of a TV presenter, but of a monster. If only her fans could see her now. But there was nothing she could do to us. She was outnumbered, and her gun was empty, but as she strode purposely in our direction, I had the feeling she was up to something.

When she was no more than a couple of feet in front of us, she pulled her hand back. A jet of orange light pushed right past Orin's force field and knocked us off our feet.

I fell hard on my ass, my tailbone exploding in pain. Orin tumbled down the stairs. But I couldn't focus on him right now, for one thought resounded through my mind. Fuck!. She could do magic?

She pulled back her hand to strike again, but I didn't

have Orin's force field to protect me. Determination flooded me. If this bitch could do magic, so could I. I'd had enough. Enough of her and enough of this bullshit.

When her burst of orange flame came for me, I was ready. I'd gathered my magic pets to me, and after ducking and rolling out of the way of her strike, I sent everything at her. Everything I had. Water, fire, air, earth. Beside me, I could feel Orin joining his magic with mine in a powerful blow—a molten geyser of elements that knocked her off her feet. Her body tumbled backward in a tangle of limbs, her head hitting the stone floor hard. She came to a stop against the base of the pulsing obelisk, one arm contorted in an unnatural manner.

I approached her cautiously, my hands out, ready for another all-out magical assault. Orin was scrambling up the stairs beside me, blood dribbling down his forehead where he must have hit his head.

Patricia was unconscious, but her body and face were morphing.

"What's happening?" I asked, backing away a step. Her skin rippled grotesquely.

Orin backed up a step too. "She's had years of magical enhancements, thanks to my mother. I guess it's wearing off. But I don't know why."

"Maybe your magic is similar to your mother's," I speculated. "So your attack triggered some sort of unraveling of her spells."

"That's a fair theory," Orin's tone sounded impressed, but I couldn't look away from the horror before me. As we watched, her blonde hair turned a dull grey, and the buttons on her dress popped as her waistline expanded. Wrinkles appeared on her forehead, and her skin sagged. I was about to open my mouth to make a comment about her not winning any sexiest People awards next year when a pain rippled through me, seizing my body in its grasp.

A bellow escaped from Orin, matching my cry as I doubled over, gasping for breath. Every movement was agony. I gingerly turned my pounding head to see King Obanstone's polished leather boots summit the steps. The ornamental dagger was clutched in his fist. "I just need a human. I suppose she'll do."

28

———

I fell to my knees, fighting against the roaring pain. I thought I might black out. "What...are you..."

"I've had enough of your tomfoolery. I'll admit, I never thought you'd last this long, but I'm not going to let the two of you foil everything I've worked for all these years. It's time you understand where you belong. Cowering on the floor." He tightened the fingers in his other hand, forming a fist, and the pain exploded through me, filling every pore. I fell to the ground as a scream ripped from me, unable to do anything but writhe in torment.

Some dim part of me was aware of the rest of the chamber, Orin gasping next to me and Tristam, his face bloodied, thrashing on one of the steps just feet below us. The king raised his hands and the knife aloft, speaking in a loud chant, no doubt mirrored at four other anchor points around Faerwild.

Orin's hand crept towards mine, his fingers grasping. At least when the world ended, we'd be together. I rallied my effort, focusing all my strength and will into my arm—my hand. Stretching it out to meet his fingers.

When our fingers met and wound through each other, something strange happened. The pain lessened. My mind cleared just a touch. As if our power together had more of a chance of resisting the king's magic.

A desperate idea seized me, and I reached back with a groan of anguish, moving my other arm to grasp for Tristam's hand. My fingers just brushed against his but fell short —he was too far. But that brush was enough. The pain had lessened for an instant, proving my theory correct. I redoubled my efforts and grabbed for Tristam's hand, locking fingers with him.

Blessed relief flooded through me as the three of us locked our hands. Sophia was lying on the stone just a few feet from Orin, a puddle of blood beneath her, her skin wan. She had passed out, but her chest still moved in a shallow rhythm. Orin seemed to understand what I was doing, and so, he inched the other way, reached out, and grabbed her wrist.

The king raised the dagger now and plunged it down into Patricia's chest. I scrunched my eyes closed to block the sight of the blow. Even awful Patricia didn't deserve to be sacrificed like some damsel in an *Indiana Jones* movie.

Sophia stirred, her eyes opening, blinking at us. We didn't have much time. Patricia's blood was wetting the foundation of the altar, the space beneath the MED detonator. "Together," I whispered through the pain, turning first to Orin, then to Tristam. They both nodded.

I went inside myself, looking for the magic version of me, the creatures Orin had taught me represented my magic. And I found more. Magic purple bunnies hopped, shimmering blue fish swam through the air, a hawk dipped and cried. A shimmering red dragon with eyes like Sophia's. A purple version of Orin stood in the vast black space inside, looking at me with determination. I gathered all the forces to me, pulling them into one huge ball of magical bad-assery. Powerful enough to defeat the most powerful magician in Faerwild. Powerful enough to stop a mad king.

Through the pain, I honed my focus. And then I hurdled that ball of magic at him with every ounce of strength I had. The strength of four.

It ripped from me with the force of a rocket launcher, striking the king square between the shoulders. Flames of purple and blue and orange and red exploded around him, whirling in a magic tornado that enveloped him.

I thought I heard his scream through the roar of the magic, but I couldn't see him inside our assault—couldn't know if he was fighting back. If it would be enough.

Until the pain inside me vanished. The tension melted from me, and my head fell to the ground in blessed relief. Whatever spell the king had placed on us had ceased.

Our magical inferno dimmed too, the flames growing faint, and then puffing away into smoke. The chamber was quiet and still. A body thumped to the ground, collapsing like a sack of potatoes. The king.

Every cell in my body protesting, I pushed to my knees, crawling towards the prone form of King Vale Obanstone. He was singed and smoking.

"Is he alive?" I croaked.

It was Tristam who turned him over. The king's eyes were closed, his unnaturally handsome face laced through with tiny black lines. "I don't think so," Tristam said, his voice strangled.

It was then that the sound of boots reached my ears, from the tunnel where we'd first entered this crypt of hell. I turned towards the entrance sluggishly. I didn't think I had it in me to fight whatever was coming out of that darkness.

My body was raw and ragged, my head roaring from the strain of releasing that much magic.

Orin didn't seem to care either, he was focusing on Sophia, holding his hands over her wound, plying her with purple quora magic. I didn't know how he had any juice left. But I hoped he could save her.

Tristam stood and held out a hand for me. His face was pale. I looked from him to his hand before taking it, grateful for help getting up to my shaky legs. "Someone's coming," he said simply. I think he might have been in shock.

I nodded, doing my best to brace myself.

Men in black SWAT uniforms poured out of the tunnel, and I risked a hope. One turned, and I saw the ICCF logo across his back. Had the cavalry arrived?

When I saw Cass with her blonde ponytail, I let out a sob of relief, my knees almost failing me. Tristam put his arm around me, keeping me from falling until Cass vaulted up the stairs and wrapped her arms around me.

We rocked back and forth, and I leaned into her strength, her presence. "I thought I'd lost you," she murmured into my shoulder. "I was so scared. I thought we'd never get here in time."

"I was a little worried about that myself."

We peeled apart reluctantly, and Cass turned to take in the scene. Two ICCF members were kneeling by Sophia, one with pointed ears taking over for Orin. Cass's eyes fixed on the king's still form. "How'd you do it? How'd you defeat him?"

I looked at Tristam. "We had a little help. Turns out all Obanstones aren't murderous bastards."

"You're telling me," Cass said with a secret smile, and it was then that Tristam caught sight of his brother, his golden hair standing out against his black uniform and bulletproof vest.

"Auberon?" Tristam breathed, stepping forward. "It's really you? She told me you were alive...but...I can't believe Father lied this whole time..." He stumbled over his words, his blue eyes wide.

Auberon strode to meet his brother and pulled him into an embrace. "We've lots to catch up on little brother. I'm happy to hear you chose the right side."

"Better late than never," Tristam said sheepishly.

"Agreed."

Tristam turned to regard Sophia. I could see his eyes sliding over the spot where his father's corpse lay prone and still. "Will she be all right?"

"The ICCF has the best doctors and healers either side of the Hedge. We'll fix her up," Auberon said.

Tristam shook his head. "I can't believe you're really here."

Orin came to stand by me, and I leaned into him. The adrenaline was draining from us, and I was starting to feel like I had been fed through a wood-chipper. "Can we get out of here?" I asked him. I didn't want to be in this place anymore, with Patricia's foreign form, gazing up with vacant eyes—the king's blackened skin beside her.

"Of course," Cass said. "You two need to get checked out too. The ICCF can handle clean up here. We're getting reports from our other teams at the other anchor points that the other Brotherhood members have been apprehended, and the MEDs recovered."

"Good." I closed my heavy eyelids for a moment, and it was a struggle to open them again.

We started toward the tunnel entrance. "Oh, just a moment," Orin said. He limped across the chamber and bent to retrieve something at the base of the stairs. When he returned, he handed it to Cass. It was the other mirror she had given us at the beginning of the trial. "What's that for?" I asked.

"How did you think we knew you were here?" Cass asked as we moved slowly into the darkness of the tunnel, back toward the altar. "Orin opened his mirror and left it on. I was smart enough not to say anything to expose the trick. Jacq, I'm so sorry about that, by the way. If I hadn't said something when you tried to contact me—"

I waved away her apology. "Water under the bridge."

She bit her lip in an expression that said that she would definitely owe me for all time, but she continued. "The mirrors have trackers, but the upstairs of the temple was empty. We were confused and couldn't find you until Orin called and left the mirror running. We were able to figure out based on the image we could see through the mirror and the king's comments where you were. So we came down here."

"Smarty-pants," I looked at Orin with fondness.

"That's Mr. Smarty-pants to you," he replied.

"We recorded all the king's comments in audio. The truth of Vale Obanstone and the Brotherhood will soon be public knowledge. The ICCF will be able to make sure nothing like this ever happens again."

"I'm glad," I said.

"It's time someone honorable rules Faerwild," Cass said.

I nodded, thinking of Tristam, but I realized that she was gazing at Auberon, her eyes shining with love.

"Oh, damn, your boyfriend is gonna be king," I said, realizing. Auberon was the elder son, so he was the heir. "Does that mean you're going to be queen? A real freaking faerie queen?"

"Jacq," Cass said, blushing.

But Auberon just put his arm around Cass, pulling her close and pressing a kiss to the side of her forehead. "Maybe someday."

I grinned at her and then turned to Orin. I planted my own kiss on his cheek. Who would have thought that both of these Montana girls would end up with faeries? Mom and Dad were going to freak.

29

The world spun around me—my only anchor, Orin's hand fixed firmly in mine. Tens of thousands of screams greeted us as we summited the stairs leading up to the stage. Most of the crowd were faeries, but some were humans, let into Faerwild just for this. The Fantastic Faerie Race award ceremony. And we were the winners.

Orin and I walked towards the two seats in the center of the huge stage, the spotlights intense above us. We weren't alone, though. The other contestants had been invited back as had Gabe and Evaline. My parents and Orin's parents waved at us from the side of the stage as we followed the other contestants, who had taken their seats in two semicircles to the left and right of our chairs.

Last to take the stage before us, Tristam was helping Sophia navigate to her seat with her crutches. It turned out she had broken her ankle after all, but I'd heard she'd landed a very lucrative modeling contract that would start once her leg healed—which would be just another day, thanks to faerie magic. It was a far cry from the future she'd almost had, just two days prior—sacrificed to the late King Vale Obanstone's greed and ambition. Even though Tristam and Sophia had gotten to the final checkpoint at the same time as us, the FFR producers had declared Orin and me the victors of the race after Tristam admitted the extent to which his father had gone to rig the race in their favor. As he sat on the couch now, one arm splayed over the back of the couch behind Sophia, Tristam looked content. I would have thought the death of his father would have left him more troubled, but he seemed almost... peaceful. As if the Faerie king's death had freed him somehow.

When Orin and I sat down, the noise of the crowd almost deafened me. The new presenter settled into the chair next to us—and this one I trusted a bit more than Patricia. My roommate, Christine, had jumped at the chance at Patricia's old job and had finally forgiven me for drinking all her whiskey after I put her name forward for the opportunity.

I surveyed the other sofas, filled with Dulcina, Molly, Duncan, and the rest. I could hardly conceive all that we'd been through together. All we'd survived. Though not everyone had made it out safely, I thought with a pang of sorrow. Behind us, two giant screens showed pictures of Zee and Genevieve. I thought of Ben, too, who had saved us at the end of the Elemental Trial. His photo should be up there too. I'd never forget what he'd sacrificed for me.

Besides our fallen friends, the only people I felt were missing from this ceremony were Cass and Auberon. I wished they could be here to see this, but I understood how busy they'd been between rounding up the Brotherhood and Auberon coming forward and presenting himself as the surprise heir to the throne who was very much alive. Plus, we would see them later.

"Jacq and Orin," Christine gushed into the microphone as the crowd finally settled down, and we turned our attention to her. Orin's fingers laced through mine, not letting go. The crowd went wild again, and many held up banners with our names and hearts drawn on them. "Congratulations you two."

I couldn't help but grin. Even after all that had happened, we had done it. We had won.

"Gabe," Christine started, turning to the couch where Gabe and Evaline sat, Gabe, looking a bit uncomfortable in a charcoal suit. "We all knew Jacq was a hero right from the start, but did you ever think she'd win?"

Gabe looked over at me and winked. "I knew she had it in her. Not many people would climb a fence to rescue someone in the middle of an audition, but Jacq did. She showed us she was special right from the start."

I felt my blush rise as the picture of Zee disappeared off the big screen to be replaced by me saving the exec's daughter from the crocodile during the last audition. Beside me, I felt Orin shift in his seat. I'd gone in because he'd left her. I knew for a fact that he regretted his judgment that day.

"Jacq continued in the same spirit throughout, putting everyone else first," continued Gabe. "I don't usually pick favorites, but I'm going to let you in on a secret. Jacq was mine right from the get-go."

"I think she's many of your favorite, too," Christine said, turning her attention back to the crowd, who roared in reply. "But it wasn't really the monsters or the challenges that made people turn their TV's on every night. It was the blossoming love story between Jacq and Orin. Let's have a recap, shall we? We all knew when these two were paired together that there would be fireworks. We just didn't know what kind."

Once again, I turned to the huge screen, wishing I could hide the flush on my cheeks. The shot came up of me picking Orin as my partner—both of our faces looked positively green at the thought. It was difficult to tell who was glaring at who more. I looked back at him, and his face was soft. I tried to remember how I'd first seen him—how I'd thought that he was anything other than the complicated, capable male who loved so deeply, once you had the privilege of getting past his walls.

The montage continued and segued into various moments from the Sorcery Trial—our argument whether or not to follow the nymphs to the Erl-king's castle, and then onto our climb down the cliff where I had to pass Orin by pressing right up against him.

"That's when I knew," Orin whispered in my ear, sending a delicious shiver down my spine.

When had I first known I had feelings for Orin? I couldn't answer the question, but it had crept up on me slowly. I'd fallen hopelessly in love with him without even trying, without even really knowing what was happening.

I gripped his hand tighter as the montage continued, right to the kiss we shared in the shadows of the alley in Elfame. So we had been caught on camera after all. The noise the crowd made was thunderous as the screen faded to black.

Christine held the microphone to my face. "Inquiring minds want to know. What did you do to grab this hotty?"

Before I had the chance to speak, Orin leaned in and answered for me. "She saved me in every possible way there is to be saved. She's my best friend, and I wouldn't want anyone else by my side when the going gets rough."

I felt my eyes begin to well up as he gripped my hand tighter.

"Plus, did you see her in that gown at the Slyph palace?" His dark eyes softened as he looked at me, his irises black as ink. "I didn't have a chance."

The crowd laughed as I playfully elbowed him.

Pulling the microphone towards me, I began to speak, needing to keep it light, playful. I didn't want the world to see the truth of what Orin meant to me. That was for him and me alone. "Did I ever tell you about the time when I saw Orin taking a bath? He thought I wasn't watching but..."—I let the sentence hang in the air.—"I peeked. Ladies, let me tell you, he's got it goin' on under all that Lycra."

The crowd roared. Some wolf whistled. Christine swiveled her eyes up and down and gave me the thumbs up. "Hot bodies aside," she said, straightening. "These past few weeks have been a very trying time. We all now know that the race was part of a terrorist plot by the late king Oban-stone to bring down the barriers between the human and faerie worlds. You also know that the ICCF is now doing everything it can to open the portals between our realms so that citizens of both worlds can intermingle safely. What you may not know, what the papers haven't told you, is that Jacq and Orin were integral to foiling the king's plan. They made sacrifices so that humans and faeries can live side by side. In peace."

Hushed whispers flooded through the crowd as Christine continued. "Now there's something that our contestants don't know. Jacq, Orin, can you stand and come with me?"

I looked at Orin, who just shrugged. We stood and followed Christine to the side of the stage. She draped her arm around my shoulder. "Jacq has been my friend for a very long time. There is no one who deserves this more than she does. The king's boon was promised as a prize for the winners, but the late King Obanstone will be unable to fulfill his promise..."

Behind her, I could see my mom waving frantically at me, a huge smile splitting her face. The loss of the boon didn't bother me, not really. I didn't need it anymore. I'd found Cass and Orin's parents were free. Auberon had released them from their indenture to house Obanstone within hours of his father's death. Orin and I had accomplished what we set out to do.

"But there is the small matter of the million dollar prize. Even though Vale Obanstone had other plans, the Fantastic Faerie Race producers and the studio have promised to keep up their end of the bargain. Ladies and gentlemen, please welcome to the stage, Jacq's former boss and the organizer of the Fantastic Faerie Race, John Ashton."

I brought my hand up to my mouth as John walked up to the stage, carrying a briefcase. In his other hand, he held a cardboard coffee cup

"I think it's about time I gave you this," he said, handing me the coffee with a smile. I took it, stunned. "I certainly owe it to you for everything you've done." Then, to my complete shock, he pulled me into a hug and whispered in my ear. "Tom Cruise has increased his offer to fifteen million!"

"Thanks," I whispered back, patting him awkwardly, "But Tom will have to find another leading lady." He appeared disappointed as he pulled back, but his smile was back in force when he saw the cameras on him. He opened the briefcase and pulled out two oversized checks. One for me and one for Orin. Each had one million dollars written on it underneath our names. I couldn't keep my hand from shaking as I took that piece of paper.

"There's one more surprise," Christine said, pulling John out of the spotlight. "Even though one of these individuals is getting ready for his own big day tomorrow, the eyes of Earth and Faerwild are on you two today."

Tears welled in my eyes as Cass and Auberon came onto the stage. Cass's smile was as bright and huge as I'd ever seen it. Each held a red velvet cushion. On the one held by Cass was a beautiful tiara. Auberon's held a crown.

I let the tears fall as Cass held the tiara over my head. "I now declare the winners of the Fantastic Faerie Race. My beautiful sister, Jacqueline Cunningham, and the equally gorgeous Orin Treebaum."

The crowd went wild as the crown and tiara were placed on our heads.

"One day you'll be the one wearing a crown," I whispered as she pulled me into a hug.

"And I wouldn't be able to if it wasn't for you."

Our embrace tightened around us as my mom and dad rushed onto the stage. The hug got bigger as Orin's parents joined us, and then Auberon. It was the first Cunningham-Treebaum-Obanstone hug ever, and I hoped it was the first of many. I was crushed in the middle of the people I loved the most, and as the tears fell, I knew there was nowhere else I'd rather be.

30

———

We sat for another hour as Christine peppered all of the FFR contestants with questions and showed us clip after clip from each of the trials. It pleased me somehow that there were moments the cameras hadn't captured. Like Orin and my first real conversation where we bared our secrets to each other. Our first kiss. My reunion with Cass and Orin's with his mother. And the death of King Vale Obanstone. There were things that belonged only in our memories. Things that belonged only to us.

Auberon was throwing a celebration for all the race contestants and our families, so we made our way to the Elfame palace when the award ceremony was complete. It was strange to regard it now—the soaring spires and towers no longer looked threatening and sinister. They looked hopeful. It was the start of a new reign. Auberon's coronation ceremony was scheduled for tomorrow morning. It meant change for Faerwild and Earth. Auberon Obanstone was not his father. And he would be a very different kind of king.

The past few days had been a whirlwind with the ICCF cleaning up the mess the Faerie king had left, debriefing us about what had happened inside that cavern, and the race producers declaring us the winners. I was still a little hoarse from my parents' reunion with Cass, I hadn't thought I had that many tears in me, but they'd flowed freely as our family was made whole for the first time in two years.

Now, Orin and I walked hand in hand up the steps of the palace. Our fathers walked to the right of us, where I heard my dad telling Orin's father about the size of the elk you can hunt in Montana. To our left, Ramona was pointing out a peculiarity of faerie architecture to my mother, whose eyes were bright with excitement. I knew Orin'd had a serious talk with his parents the first chance they'd had to be alone, and his parents had confirmed that Niall was a liar, trying to unsettle Orin with what he'd said when he'd been tied up at the house. Orin's parents had never sent him away, it had truly been the king who had banished little Orin from the palace. They'd lost eighteen years with each other, but when I saw them together now, I could see they'd be able to make up that lost time. Now that they were a family again.

"It hardly feels real, does it," I murmured, snuggling against Orin's side.

He wrapped his arm around me. "I don't know what you're talking about. I always carry million dollar checks in my pocket," Orin joked.

"What's the first thing you're going to buy?" I asked him. I hadn't had much time to dream, but I thought mine just might be a plane ticket to Montana. I had a hankering for a few days of wide-open, starry sky and a few dozen of my mom's chocolate chip cookies.

"There's this girl that I like," Orin said, answering my question.

I raised an eyebrow as he continued. "And I realized that she and I have never been on a real date. I'd like to buy her dinner."

"I'd like that." I grinned at him.

His eyes went wide, and he grimaced. "Oh, no, did you think it was you? This is awkward—"

I pulled back from his embrace and punched him in the arm. "Har, har. The faerie thinks he's a comedian now?"

"Watching those clips from the first trial made me realize how much I miss the little death-glares you were always shooting me," he pouted.

"There's plenty where those came from," I retorted, but my next comment was cut off as we walked into the ballroom. The room's soaring ceiling and chandeliers looked like they should be watching over an enchanted gala, but the smell of barbeque and the sounds of an electric guitar greeted us instead. I raised my nose in the air and breathed in deeply, savoring the smell.

"Cass handled the catering," Auberon said, coming up to greet us. "Welcome!" I could have kissed my sister. I could go for some good barbeque.

Auberon walked us over to the bar and waited as we placed our orders. A whiskey neat for Orin, a cold beer for me. I'd been craving one for ages. When we had our drinks in hand, Auberon lifted his own. "I wanted to thank you both, officially, for all you've done. And for being so... forgiving of how my family mistreated you both, and for me taking Cass from you, Jacq."

"It's forgotten," I said warmly, meaning it. It was time to start fresh.

"I know you were promised a boon, and I don't have quite the magic that my father did in that regard. I feel bad about that," Auberon said, "so I wanted to give you something else, instead."

I started to say that wasn't necessary, but Orin elbowed me in the ribs. He was clearly curious to see what Auberon was going to gift us.

Auberon pulled two silver cards out of his jacket pocket and handed one to each of us. It was weighty in my hand, made of metal. I looked at the engraving on the card. It had my name and the ICCF logo emblazoned on the front. "What is it?"

"These two are the first of their kind. Hopefully, the first of many. They are all access visas for both Faerwild and Earth. You'll be able to travel across the Hedge between Faerwild and Earth at any time through any portal in the world without question. You two are the first official dual citizens of Faerwild and Earth."

I looked at Orin and then back to Auberon, amazement filling me. "This...this is..." But I couldn't get the words out. With these visas, Orin and I would never have to be separated, or worry about where to live. The world was our oyster. Two worlds.

Orin put a hand out, and Auberon shook it. "Thank you. This..." He seemed tongue-tied too.

"You're welcome," Auberon said, nodding. "Now, I should greet the rest of the guests and get this party started!" He held up his glass, and we clinked our own against his. It felt right to celebrate. This was the start of something wonderful.

The party lasted late into the night. Cass must have been in charge of the music too because the band who played kicked up the jams and belted out hit after hit. People flooded the dance floor—Ruth and the other camera crew members, Gabe and Evaline, Tristam and Sophia on her crutches, making happy fools of themselves, Auberon's faerie courtiers, my Mom and Dad, even John and Christine and the other race producers. Drinks flowed, and faeries and humans whirled and laughed.

I spun in and around the other contestants, stealing a mini tart from Yael with a laugh (revenge for my croissants all those weeks ago), even taking a turn around the dance floor with Ario, as he apologized for betting about Orin and me. Dulcina and Molly and Sophia and I posed for pictures, collapsing in a pile of giggles on a velvet couch. After the ruthless backstabbing, everyone seemed ebullient at the fact that we weren't enemies anymore. It felt wrong to hold grudges after what we'd all been through together. Fire-breathing dragons and hostile merfolk and possessed magic armor...not to mention all types of deadly faerie creatures. It felt better to be glad—to celebrate that we had made it through alive.

Orin watched my antics with a quiet smile, chatting with his parents and mine, laughing with the other contestants. Our eyes were always on each other, though. No matter where we found ourselves in the ballroom, I knew exactly where my dark angel was standing.

My feet were tired from dancing and my cheeks smarting from laughing by the time I made it back to him, falling into his arms.

"Why, Mr. Treebaum," I said, leaning against him. Perhaps I was slightly more tipsy than I'd realized. "May I have this dance?"

Orin threaded one hand in mine, the other around my waist, pulling me close. "There's another type of dance I'm thinking of, you know."

My senses roared to life within me at his growled

comment, and I took an inadvertent step closer. I thought I knew exactly what type of dance he was referring to.

"But...I need a piece of information first," he pulled back a touch. "I admitted earlier the first time I knew I'd fallen for you. I think you should admit the same."

"I don't know," I pretended to ponder. "I was planning to take that particular secret to my grave."

"I think I already know when it was," he said, his hand running up the arrow of my spine in a way that made my knees weak. "I just want to see if I was right."

I cast him a doubtful look. "You think you're such a Jacqueline expert? Well, shoot, professor. What is your... uneducated guess?"

"When you saw me kissing the xana," he said with a devilish grin. "I've never seen someone look so green with envy."

I huffed, my happily tipsy mind searching for a compelling lie. Because he was right. Thinking on it, that was the exact moment I'd known, for certain, that I had feelings for Orin. "I wasn't jealous she was kissing *you*," I said, fighting to keep the smile from my face. It was hopeless to try to hide it. "I just...hadn't had a good kiss in a while, that's all."

"And now?" he pulled me back close, so my body was flush against his. His lips lingered just inches from mine, as sweet and sinful as lips had ever been. I looked to the side, struggling with every fiber of my being to feign nonchalance. "I'm afraid I'm still waiting."

It was Orin's turn to scoff. "Now, who's the comedian!" He took my face in his hands, trailing the fingers of one hand down my neck, making me shiver. "I guess I'll just have to give you a kiss so epic it will ruin you for all other kisses."

I licked my lips in anticipation. "So long as it's the first of many."

Orin smiled down at me, and my heart fluttered in my chest at the loveliness of the sight. "The first of many, many, many."

And when he kissed me, the room spun around us, as if all of Faerwild itself had shifted orbit so it revolved around only us. The Fantastic Faerie Race had asked so much of us —had taken so much too. But it had given more. I had my sister back, a visa that would take me anywhere in two worlds, and a million dollars in my pocket. But the one prize that had made all the sacrifice worth it was Orin. Together, we had cried and fought and bled. As the real as the race had been, it had been fantasy, not reality.

Now, real life could begin.

ABOUT J.A. ARMITAGE

J.A lives in a total fantasy world (because reality is boring right?) When she's not writing all the crazy fun in her head, she can be found eating cake, designing pretty pictures and hanging upside down from the tallest climbing frame in the local playground while her children look on in embarrassment. She's travelled the world working as everything from a banana picker in Australia to a Pantomime clown, has climbed to the top of Mount Kilimanjaro and the bottom of the Grand Canyon and once gave birth to a surrogate baby for a friend of hers.

She spends way too much time gossiping on Facebook and if you want to be part of her Reading Army, where you'll get lots of freebies, exclusive sneak peeks and super secret sales, join up here https://www.subscribepage.com/v7o8l

ABOUT CLAIRE LUANA

Claire Luana grew up in Seattle reading everything she could get her hands on and writing every chance she could. Eventually, adulthood won out, and she turned her writing talents to more scholarly pursuits, going to work as a commercial litigation attorney.

While continuing to practice law, Claire decided to return to her roots and try her hand once again at creative writing. She has written and published four fantasy series: the Moonburner Cycle, the Confectioner Chronicles, the Knights of Caerleon (co-written with Jesikah Sundin), and The Faerie Race (co-written with J.A. Armitage).

She lives in Seattle, Washington with her husband and two dogs. In her (little) remaining spare time, she loves to hike, travel, binge-watch CW shows, and of course, fall into a good book.

Connect with Claire Luana online at:

Website & Blog: http://www.claireluana.com
Facebook: http://www.facebook.com/claireluana
Twitter: http://www.twitter.com/clairedeluana
Goodreads: https://www.goodreads.com/author/show/15207082.Claire_Luana
Instagram: http://www.instagram.com/claireluana

ALSO BY J.A. ARMITAGE

Reverse Fairytales

Charm

Lucky Charm

Charmed

Dark Water

Blue Water

Breakwater

Dragon Slayer

Slayer

Warrior

Protector

The Faerie Race

The Sorcery Trial

The Elemental Trial

The Doomsday Trial

ALSO BY CLAIRE LUANA

Moonburner Cycle

Moonburner, Book One

Sunburner, Book Two

Starburner, Book Three

Burning Fate, Prequel Novella

Confectioner Chronicles

The Confectioner's Guild, Book One

The Confectioner's Coup, Book Two

The Confectioner's Truth, Book Three

The Confectioner's Exile, Prequel Novella

The Knights of Caerleon, with Jesikah Sundin

The Fifth Knight, Book One

The Third Curse, Book Two

The First Gwenevere, Book Three

The Faerie Race

The Sorcery Trial (Faerie Race book one)

The Elemental Trial (Faerie Race book two)

The Doomsday Trial (Faerie Race book three)

Orion's Kiss